Assault

with a

Deadly Lie

Terrace Books, a trade imprint of the University of Wisconsin Press, takes its name from the Memorial Union Terrace, located at the University of Wisconsin–Madison. Since its inception in 1907, the Wisconsin Union has provided a venue for students, faculty, staff, and alumni to debate art, music, politics, and the issues of the day. It is a place where theater, music, drama, literature, dance, outdoor activities, and major speakers are made available to the campus and the community. To learn more about the Union, visit www.union.wisc.edu.

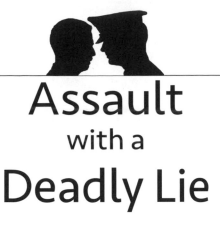

Assault
with a
Deadly Lie

A Nick Hoffman Novel of Suspense

Lev Raphael

Terrace Books
A trade imprint of the University of Wisconsin Press

Terrace Books
A trade imprint of the University of Wisconsin Press
1930 Monroe Street, 3rd Floor
Madison, Wisconsin 53711-2059
uwpress.wisc.edu

3 Henrietta Street
London WC2E 8LU, England
eurospanbookstore.com

Printed in the United States of America

Library of Congress Cataloging-in-Publication Data

Raphael, Lev, author.
Assault with a deadly lie: a Nick Hoffman novel of suspense /
Lev Raphael.
pages   cm
ISBN 978-0-299-30230-6 (cloth: alk. paper)
ISBN 978-0-299-30233-7 (e-book)
1. Hoffman, Nick (Fictitious character)—Fiction.
2. Stalking—Fiction.   3. College teachers—Fiction.
4. English teachers—Fiction.   5. Gay men—Fiction.
6. Michigan—Fiction.   I. Title.
PS3568.A5988A94   2014
813'.54—dc23
2014007468

For

Marie

and

Gene

" . . . we wallow here on the stormy sea of fortune."

Boethius

Assault

with a

Deadly Lie

1

I confess I'd been watching too much terror TV. I couldn't stop. I couldn't get enough of *24*, *NCIS*, *Homeland*, *Sleeper Cell*, *MI-5*, and *The State Within*. I watched them all. I watched the reruns and I rented the DVDs, sometimes more than once. These shows and miniseries drew me the way other people were hypnotized by the corniest disaster movies. You know, the ones with "all-star" casts and warbling theme songs.

It wasn't just because of 9/11, which had branded the calendar over a decade ago. And it's not as if I really thought anything in those shows could happen to me: kidnapping, bomb threats, torture. But I had inexplicably been involved in enough crime at the State University of Michigan (SUM) to realize that even the sanest existence—mine as a bibliographer of Edith Wharton—could be struck by lightning like a lone tree in a field, blasted and fried.

Maybe I was superstitious. My life had calmed down considerably after getting tenure, becoming a full professor, and being appointed to oversee a departmental speaker's program endowed by a former straight-A student of mine. He had made it big in a dot.com, died young of cancer, and left money in his will to the university, with me as the sole administrator. With my new status, crime and instability had disappeared from my world, and so maybe I was trying to fill it with sensationalistic visions of chaos to ward off actual chaos by sympathetic magic. I failed.

That warm late May evening, I was putting out the lights downstairs in our typical 1950s Michiganapolis center hall Colonial. It was a beautiful house on a street where the maples grew so thick and tall that their foliage formed a canopy over the street from spring into the fall. There was always something mildly ceremonial when you drove along it in the warm, green months.

I'd grown up in New York City—the Upper West Side specifically—as the child of immigrants, Jewish refugees from 1930s Europe. A different world entirely: brownstones, massive apartment buildings, endless noise and commotion. Traffic on Broadway, traffic on Riverside Drive and West End Avenue, traffic on the West Side Highway. But it was safe despite the commotion.

Still, my Michiganapolis home had seemed an even stronger bulwark against the kind of horror my parents had survived by fleeing and building a very comfortable life in America. Yes, my cousin Sharon lovingly derided where I lived as very *Father Knows Best*, but that was okay by me. If you can't indulge in fantasy in your own home, you might as well never buy a house, and as fantasies go, it was pretty tame. But then what would you expect of a bibliographer? We don't dream of winning literary prizes, we just hope nobody finds an error in our indexes and gloats about it in print. As writers go, we're not fierce and stately wolves, we're more like prairie dogs ducking down into our tunnels at the first sign of threat.

At least that's what I thought.

As I turned off the last lamp in our spacious blue and gold living room, the kind of relaxed, cozy room that would sell a house even in a bad real estate market, I could see flashing lights in the distance through the nearest window. Two black armored personnel carriers hurtled down our quiet Michiganapolis street, and I wasn't shocked as much as resigned. I'd seen the SWAT team vehicles in our local newspaper in an article about "domestic preparedness," but never in action of any kind.

"This is it," I thought. There were terrorists in our college town. *On my street.* Of course. It had to happen. We were an unlikely target, which made it all the more possible.

And then the APCs shuddered to a stop right in front of our house.

That's when I started to panic, and felt rooted to the living room window, even though a voice inside me shouted "Run!" Upstairs, out the back, anywhere. Run.

My throat tightened, my face felt icy cold despite the balmy air bringing in the rich scent of lilacs and viburnums from the front and back yards. In novels, people's stomachs are always churning when they face the worst, but I felt paralyzed from the neck down, hell, from the neck up, too. I couldn't speak, I couldn't blink, I could barely breathe.

The APC doors burst open and a dozen men encased in black combat boots, black uniforms, kneepads, helmets, ski masks, and body armor surged across our yard like some crazy little tidal wave. They carried MP-5 submachine guns, pointed slightly down, but I knew from what I'd read that their fingers were on the triggers—just in case. I flashed on the opening of Matt Damon's disaster movie *Hereafter*. If the whole house had been rocked off its foundation right then, and swept down the street by a giant wall of water, if I had started to drown, I would not have been surprised.

I *was* drowning. In fear.

Someone pounded on the door, shouting, and I could make out two words: "police" and "warrant." Lights flashed on all up and down the street with the frenzy of paparazzi outside the hottest new club, and still I couldn't move. I felt as weirdly distant as if I were having a near-death experience, hovering above my body on a hospital table, surrounded by doctors, machines, all of it laboring to keep me alive, to bring me back.

My partner Stefan rushed down the stairs from our bedroom at the back of the house, wearing only thin cotton pajama pants. "Is there a fire? What happened?" He was squinting and looked half-asleep. He clearly hadn't seen or heard the APCs pull up.

He stepped to the door and before I could say anything, he opened it.

"Stefan Borowski? We have a warrant to search this house." There was more, but I couldn't take in the words that were being barked at him as if he were an inmate in a prison camp being ordered to his knees for execution. Teams of cops shot off into the house like hunting dogs on the scent of prey.

Others surrounded him. At least half a dozen of the black-clad warriors dragged him out onto the front lawn and I thought with horrible clarity: "They're going to kill him and me and I'll never know why." He didn't resist—how could he?—but then neither did I when it was my turn. As a handful of the SWAT team headed toward me, I felt very small and weak. Their guns, belts, badges, helmets, and masks seemed to swell up like portents in a nightmare. I was too shocked to do anything as I felt myself lifted up and almost hurled out of my own house onto the freshly cut grass.

Someone held me down and if I hadn't been breathless, I would have started to cry. I couldn't see anything but the grass in front of my eyes, and my face felt weirdly cold and hot at the same time. Behind me, through what must have been the open door, I heard men stomping up and down the stairs. The smell of the grass was overpowering, it made me even dizzier than I was already, and for a moment I thought I might pass out, but I knew I had to stay alert. Somehow. The sting of the cold, cut grass on my face helped.

My arms were yanked behind me and I could hear and feel handcuffs being clamped onto my wrists, unbelievably cold and frightening. My shoulders started to ache.

I tried to turn my head to see where Stefan was lying stretched out and a bass voice close to my ear growled, "Keep the fuck down or I will crush your fucking skull, *faggot*." I couldn't tell exactly where the cop was standing or how many of our neighbors were out on the street staring at the bizarre spectacle, but there must have been some gawkers because the same ugly voice started ordering people away and back into their houses. "Police business! Get the fuck out of here! And you—no cameras!"

I couldn't tell you if time stood still or sped up or entirely disappeared. All I know is that I had never before felt so terrified and alone, and for the first time I understood the awful lines from *King Lear* about man being a poor, forked creature. There was no raging storm around me, no thunder, wind or rain. But there might as well have been.

I wanted to call out to Stefan, but I was too cowardly to speak, and the shame of that made me wish they *had* killed me.

And then, something even more bizarre happened, if that were possible.

"Officer, my name is Vanessa Liberati. I'm an attorney and I represent these men. What's going on here? May I see your warrant?"

I recognized the Brooklyn-accented voice from her first word, which sounded almost like "Orfficuh." Vanessa was our new neighbor from across the street, and she was known in Michiganapolis as one of the city's best defense lawyers. She was pure New York. There was a steely edge to her questions now that filled me with wild hope: cast-iron fist in an ultra-suede glove. We barely knew each other, since she'd moved in just a few months ago, so her appearing on our lawn felt like a *deus ex machina*.

"Are these men being arrested? Where are you taking them? Can you at least let them sit up? They're clearly unarmed."

But I didn't want to sit up, I didn't want anyone to see my face. I wanted to sink into the ground and never emerge. I felt horribly exposed. What would my neighbors think? That I was a drug dealer, for sure.

"Stay calm and don't say anything," Vanessa said to me *sotto voce*, and she must have gone over to talk to Stefan, who lay I don't know how many feet away. I heard her give her spiel again to another cop, I guess. She returned and crouched by my side. "I will take care of this. You're gonna be fine. Just relax."

There was something almost hypnotic in her assurance, and crazily, I did start to feel less freaked out.

I managed to move my head a bit and peered up at her. Tall, slim, green-eyed and freckled, with masses of pre-Raphaelite auburn hair, she was wearing a form-fitting black suit that made her look like she'd stepped right out of a courtroom, though it was much too late at night for that.

Vanessa winked at me, and then nodded as if to remind me to keep quiet. She stood up.

"Who's the officer in charge?" she asked loudly, as if challenging him to personal combat. Someone told her, "Detective Quinn. He's back at the station." I heard her start making calls, softly, and from what I could hear, it seemed she was getting someone to cover her court schedule for the next day.

This was what it must be like, I thought, to have made it off a sinking ship and after weeks in a lifeboat, finally see hope on the horizon. I was so helpless, she seemed almost godlike. Nobody was insulting her or ordering her around, and that in itself gave me the stirrings of confidence.

"I'm going inside," she told me and I may have passed out briefly or fallen asleep. I came to when her hand touched my shoulder and she said, "I don't know what they were looking for, but they haven't found anything. They're taking your partner in, it's standard procedure. But they're letting you go. I'll follow him to the county jail. You make some coffee and wait for me, it's going to be a long night. I left my cell number on your kitchen counter. I promise I'll get your partner back to you *pronto.*"

And she was right about them not taking me off. A SWAT team goon uncuffed me and let me back into my house. One of the black APCs was gone, and so was Stefan. I shut the front door behind me and fell to my knees shaking, because all I could imagine was that I'd never see him again, despite Vanessa's assurances. And then our Westie puppy, Marco, appeared from wherever he'd been hiding during the onslaught and started climbing up me to lick my face. He seemed remarkably unperturbed, but as always, tuned right in to how I was feeling.

I was profoundly ashamed: How had I forgotten him in the attack? I scooped him up into my arms and made a slow circuit of both floors to see the damage. I expected a whirlwind of destruction, books flung from shelves, couches, chairs, and mattresses ripped open—you know, like in the movies—but there were only a few lamps knocked over, some pictures askew, as if the cops had merely bumped into things in their frantic search—for what? It couldn't be drugs. We were both harmless academics; Stefan was the university's writer-in-residence.

There was no reason to target us for an attack like this.

I put Marco down, and everywhere we went in the house I had once thought was so beautiful, I turned on lights. Darkness would have chilled me. And with each flicked switch, I felt the shock all over again of armed, hostile invaders stomping through my house, ripping the quiet fabric of my life to shreds. The SWAT team hadn't used tear gas, but they might as well have. My eyes stung no matter where I looked.

Marco was always eager and curious, and he trotted after me now as if we were playing a new kind of game. Though he was a rescue dog, he surprisingly did not seem at all agitated by the invasion we'd suffered, and I was glad to have him by my side at every step. When I put up a pot of coffee and also made myself a cup of espresso in the new Gaggia machine Stefan had splurged on, Marco settled down on his little dog bed and fell instantly asleep.

I wished my life could be that simple. I stared down at the notepad by the phone where Vanessa Liberati had left two numbers, home and cell, with a big "Stay calm!" scrawled underneath.

I was calm, I guess. And that scared me. The glittering kitchen with its gray-blue granite-topped island seemed as exposed as if a tornado had ripped the roof off our house and shattered everything inside. I had stopped shaking.

But I wondered if I would ever feel safe again in this house, or safe anywhere I went, no matter how far from the scene of this nightmare.

2

I drank enough coffee that night to stay awake all summer. What was happening to Stefan? Where was he? Was he in a cell? Was he being interrogated? Tortured even? Nothing seemed too crazy, too impossible.

But then I reminded myself that Vanessa was at the jail too, and would be protecting him somehow. Wouldn't she?

I sat in the kitchen, too anxious to even leave the room. I drank coffee and watched Marco breathe. Friends with kids have told me that what I've felt watching him sleep is exactly how they felt when they had infants: deep abiding wonderment and a fascination that seemed bottomless. Marco had been abused by his previous owner, and every good moment he had with us struck me as a triumph over his hateful past.

I studied him as he drifted into a dream now and then, making little "whoop-whoop" noises, his feet and tail twitching. Was he chasing a rabbit? Or was he dreaming about our home invasion? What would *my* dreams be like whenever I finally did fall asleep? Would I be able to sleep without wondering if it would happen again?

Every little noise I thought I heard in the house now made me freeze. "They're back," I thought, hoping that was nonsense, but dreading it just the same. I turned on the kitchen laptop to stream classical music. I needed something to cover the quiet that seemed ominous.

They were playing Rachmaninov, a cello trio, and its fierce mournfulness couldn't have fit the moment any better.

I had never felt so alone before. I thought of calling my cousin Sharon in New York because she was like a sister to me. Over the years, we had often spoken to each other in the middle of the night when trouble squeezed us in its fist. But this all seemed so alien, so incomprehensible, I didn't think I could talk to anyone. What the hell would I say? Where would I start? *How* could I start?

I was ashamed, profoundly ashamed and couldn't bear the thought of opening up that wound even to Sharon. I hadn't done anything, yet I felt the SWAT team had humiliated me, stripped me of my dignity forever. How could I drive down our street again or even take out my trash? People would be staring at me, whispering about me and Stefan, speculating as to what had brought the police to our house and violated the peace of one of Michiganapolis's prettiest neighborhoods.

So I sat there, in a black hole, shrinking deeper and deeper into myself until Vanessa called around 4 a.m. from the jail to say that Stefan wasn't being charged, and that she was bringing him home shortly. "We'll discuss everything when I get there."

I took that to mean she didn't want anyone overhearing what she said. And that was okay. I eked out a few words of thanks, hung up and waited. I had no idea where or how far away the jail was.

Nothing made sense to me. It was as if some internal mechanism of gravity had failed and my thoughts drifted in every direction. No, it was much worse than that. I myself was drifting, as helpless as the astronaut in *2001: A Space Odyssey* who's been cut loose by Hal. I was surrounded by a void and would never be safe again.

I'm not religious, I didn't curse at God and ask how something so awful could happen to me and Stefan. But I couldn't stop reflecting on how my life, our lives, had been almost uniformly positive for six straight years (except for one of Stefan's students killing himself about a year ago). Stefan had written a best-selling memoir about his surprising conversion from Judaism to Catholicism; I was no longer at the bottom of the heap in my Department of English, American Studies, and Rhetoric (EAR); my elderly parents were healthy; and Sharon's cancer continued to be in remission. We had a good solid life, a well-behaved dog—none of it was the stuff of drama, and I liked that. I enjoyed teaching my classes, working on inviting the yearly guest writer to SUM, taking car trips to Lake Michigan or into Canada. I had never imagined I could be happy anywhere else but New York City, yet here I was, contented, rooted, at home.

And now all of that seemed burned to ash. I thought of one of Stefan's favorite quotes from a Polish poet born Jewish, Antoni Slominski: "Behind the stage of our life, concealed in the wings, great factories of suffering are at work that will visit us one day."

I heard a car pull into the driveway and rushed to the front door to let them in. I gasped when Stefan emerged from Vanessa's orange Nissan Murano. I had somehow forgotten that the police had dragged him off just as he was: barefoot and half-naked. Pale, shoulders drooping, he looked haggard and hollowed-out standing next to Vanessa, who was as elegant in her fitted suit and Louboutins as if she were headed to a cocktail party at the governor's mansion. The contrast between them was devastating.

As Stefan approached the threshold, and I reached out to hug him, he brushed past me and headed wearily to the stairs. Marco had come out of the kitchen and was wagging his tail sleepily as he watched Stefan's progress.

"I don't want to talk about it," Stefan said, voice on the edge of breaking, and there was a sharp note of warning in his voice. But how could I back off?

Vanessa grabbed my arm and said quietly, "Don't. This is the worst time. I told him to take a couple of Valium and go to sleep. He needs oblivion more than anything else right now. Trust me. I've seen it before. Lots."

I relented, closed the door and led her into the kitchen, Marco following us. He sniffed her shoes and then went back to his little bed and was almost instantly asleep again. What a gift that was.

Vanessa glanced around admiringly, taking in the antiqued glass-doored cabinets, the granite backsplashes, the appliance garages. She was keen-eyed and clearly adding it all up in her head. I didn't mind, it didn't feel intrusive or predatory, and I half expected her to ask a New York question about how much the house cost. Watching her, I was even more astonished that she looked fresh and energized after hours at the jail.

"She *loves* this," I thought, not exactly sure what "this" was. Vanessa reminded me of my cousin Sharon whose first career had been modeling—she had a similar sense of style and her posture was intimidatingly perfect.

"May I?" she said, walking right over to the coffee pot. She helped herself to a cup as if we were old friends, or at least longtime neighbors. That also struck me as very New York, and I think I smiled. A New

Zealand friend once told me that New Yorkers say, "Can I have a look at that?" and reach for whatever it is, while where she came from, you'd ask the question and wait as long as it took for you to get permission.

Vanessa sat down at the island, waved me to a bar stool across from her, and started. "Okay, here's the deal. I know you didn't ask me to get involved, but when I saw the gorillas show up across the street from me, I knew you needed help."

"What do you mean?"

"I'm from Brooklyn, okay? I'm not one of these Midwest nimrods. So I see two nice gay guys who teach at the university, love their puppy to death, never bother their neighbors—no way they'd be thugs. Believe me, I know thugs, I was married to one, and I've defended my share."

"You knew we were gay?"

"Puh-leeze. Two guys, one house, gorgeous landscaping? What else would you be? But forget about you being drug dealers or terrorists. Not in this lifetime."

"Wait—is that what happened? They were really looking for drugs? Or bombs?" I couldn't believe I was even asking questions like that in my own home. It was one more sign of how I had been scraped right out of my normal life like an oyster being shucked from its shell.

"That was my first thought, but I knew right away whatever reason they were there had to be bullshit. I've seen your partner at Mass at St. Jude's, and I can tell he's a decent guy. I'm a pretty good judge of character, you have to be when you're a defense attorney."

Stefan had never mentioned that Vanessa went to the Catholic church he'd joined after his conversion, but then we mostly spoke about the homilies more than the people there. I suppose that was natural; he's a writer and words moved him in unique ways.

"Would you have intervened if you knew we were guilty—of something?"

"Hey! Everybody deserves a defense, even criminals. That's the law until they change it. Okay, Nick—It's Nick, right? Not Nicky or Nicolas? Okay, then. All of us defense attorneys have contacts on the force. We cultivate them, we have to. So here's what little I've found out: The police got an anonymous tip that someone was being held hostage here, and guns were involved."

"Are you kidding me? Who would we hold hostage? A reviewer who trashed one of Stefan's books? That's insane! And we've never had a gun in our lives." I didn't add that back before my life had returned to normal, I'd felt so threatened on campus that I'd gone to a gun shop and considered buying one. I'd actually made two trips, but in the end couldn't overcome my own queasiness about giving in to my fear.

Vanessa shrugged. "A tip's a tip. They take all of that seriously. They have to. And they have to justify their existence," she added sourly. She pulled her rippling auburn curls up off the back of her neck and then let them drop.

"What are you talking about?"

She sipped her coffee and shrugged. "You must not read the news much. The country's lousy with SWAT teams. They roll 'em out for everything from domestic disputes to serving an ordinary warrant. Every little Podunk town in America *has* one or *wants* one."

"But where do they get the money? I thought we were just barely out of a recession."

She finished her coffee and went to get herself some more. I liked the way she made herself at home here. I also liked that she was tough; that gave me courage, brought me out of myself enough to stop feeling so lost.

"Are you hungry?" I asked, trying to imagine what you would eat at a time like this.

"Coffee's fine. Very smooth."

"It's Dallmayr from Munich." I loved how she pronounced the word as "cawfee." My own New York accent had faded somewhat over the years, and so had Stefan's, thanks to a few years of teaching in Massachusetts.

Leaning back against the rounded granite counter edge, she said, "The Pentagon unloads tons of surplus material on local police forces, millions of dollars of stuff every year."

"Is that legal?"

"The laws have been changing and nobody notices, nobody really cares. The military's training cops, too, which is worse. Soldiers crush the enemy, cops are supposed to keep people safe. Those aren't compatible missions. It means people like you—and me—we're not citizens anymore. We're the enemy. And it's only gonna get worse because the more ex-soldiers go into the police, the more regular cops think they're soldiers."

"I don't believe that."

Vanessa set down her cup, and with a bit of asperity in her voice, said, "You were really lucky tonight. Yes, I said *lucky*. It's bad enough so many ex-soldiers are cops now, but lots of cops think they're soldiers already. And the cops in this town have a lousy reputation, let me tell you. Tampering with evidence, lying on police reports, corruption, violence. They've killed people's dogs in raids just for fun, they destroy property, you name it. I'm telling you, if they could waterboard suspects, they'd do it. Cops from other nearby jurisdictions hate them, call them the Gestapo. You got off pretty easy. They could have battered down your door or even blown it open. They could have used flashbang grenades once they got inside."

"You can't be serious. This isn't a war zone."

She paced back and forth across the kitchen. "Wake up! The whole world's a war zone now, and that includes Michiganapolis. They coulda shot you and claimed you drew a gun on them."

"I told you, we don't *own* any guns."

"So what? You'd be dead, and they'd never go to prison for doing it. Juries believe cops even over respectable citizens like you. Happens all the time. It happens *every day*." She thought a minute as if consulting some inner chart. "Well, needless raids happen every day. Dozens of them. Welcome to reality. And did they take your laptops? Your tablets? Your smart phones? Because if they had, you would never get them back. They hate lawyers and make us beg to get evidence back when a case is closed—and it can take years, seriously. It's like something out of *Bleak House*."

"You read Dickens?"

She grinned ruefully. "Never got all the way through, but every lawyer knows that book by reputation."

I confessed that I'd never gotten all the way through it, either, and I'd been an English major. Then I returned to something she'd said before. "If they didn't find a hostage and didn't find guns, why did they take Stefan with them? Why did they keep him so long?"

"Because they had a warrant. And a few hours is nothing. They could have kept him much longer, just because. The cops use tips from all kinds of crappy informants, even anonymous ones, and the judges don't hold them back the way they should. Warrants are as easy to get as herpes."

I tried to answer that, and she cut me off: "I know what you're thinking. You're a citizen, you have rights, constitutional protections." She cocked her head. "I wish that were really true, but everything's contingent now. You're only as free as they let you be. And you're lucky you live here and not in New York. They send out SWAT teams randomly there just as a show of force, to scare the shit out of people. The cops in New York have more employees than the FBI and they have weapons that can shoot down a plane if they want to. They have goddamn drone submarines. They really *are* an army. They even have their own version of the CIA."

It made a horrible kind of sense for New York, which had been attacked twice, and in a country where even President Obama claimed the right to assassinate an American citizen anywhere in the world just on the suspicion of a connection to terrorism. But I didn't want to believe Vanessa, even though I knew she couldn't be making any of it up. If she was one of the best lawyers in Michiganapolis, she couldn't have gotten that reputation by living in fantasy.

As if reading my mind, she said, "By the way, you haven't officially hired me to represent you on this case, but—"

"Represent us? You saved us!"

She grinned almost bashfully, revealing teeth worthy of a model.

"Of course I want you to represent us," I said. "So what's next?"

Then she looked very serious. "Well, your partner is going to need a lot of support now. Don't push him, just listen when he's ready to talk, and don't be surprised by anything he says. Remember, you guys are privileged white professionals, eager to please, never been in legal trouble, am I right? Life is good to you compared to most other people. So getting treated like this will hit you harder than someone growing up expecting life to bake them a shit casserole."

I knew exactly what she meant, and could tell she was speaking from bitter experience—not her own, but her clients'.

"And Nick, whatever you do, do not speak to the police, do not speak to *anyone*. They might send someone around, probing. Just refer them to me."

"Are you kidding? Why? What would they want?"

"To cover up. This was all bullshit. They'll want to keep it quiet if they can, or at least not look bad. And if they can find anything out about you somehow or get you to incriminate yourself about anything at all, bam! That makes the screw-up go away."

"Should we be worried about the phone?"

She nodded. "Definitely. You can't assume your phone isn't being tapped now. But I tend to be over-cautious about things like that. Listen, you've got that cute little dog. If you have something you and Stefan want to talk about just between you concerning this case, why not take him for a walk, or go into your backyard. Talk outdoors, that's always much safer."

"*Is* it a case?" I asked, thinking back to something she had said moments before.

"I hope not. But it might be. Like I said, I don't trust the cops in this town, they've got a really bad reputation. And one more thing, if you're social media junkies, and you're constantly letting people know where you are, like on Facebook or wherever, stop it right now."

I told Vanessa that wasn't an issue, and I walked her to the door, unsure how to express my gratitude, but that melted away when she said before stepping outside, "If they got a tip targeting you, that means somebody really hates one or both of you guys. My advice? Start thinking about who it might be, because this could happen again."

3

I didn't go upstairs to try and sleep because I was afraid of waking Stefan, and he needed sleep more than I did.

But honestly, I also didn't want to see him in his current state, awake *or* asleep. My strong, athletic partner was handsomer in middle age than he'd ever been before, and I wasn't prepared to witness his collapse. Not when I was so shattered myself. It was too shocking, too mortifying. Call it selfish, but I needed to protect myself any way I could right then, and just being around him would have unraveled me.

That made me feel even worse, even more isolated. How had I become a person who could even *think* like this?

After reluctantly turning out most of the lights, I slipped off my shoes and sacked out on one of the twin overstuffed couches in our living room whose décor seemed utterly beside the point. We'd been so proud of this room that trumpeted comfort and conviviality, but it struck me now as an utterly false invitation. This was a Potemkin Village, masking what life was really like.

I had found some melatonin in the downstairs bathroom and taken a few, but they didn't seem to be having any impact at all. I wasn't a romantic, yet I thought of Byron's sad lines that night: "in my heart / There is a vigil, and these eyes but close / To look within." I kept seeing the APCs pull up, the black uniforms, the guns, and pictured myself being dragged from the house and hurled onto the grass. Oddly, I didn't feel sore, not even in my shoulders. Maybe I was still in a state of shock and my body's messages were scrambled.

Vanessa had said it could have been worse, and I agreed, but for completely different reasons. The black-clad thugs had come at night, and hopefully at least some of our neighbors had slept through the storm. By day, it would have been much worse, since there were a number of nosy retirees on our street and stay-at-home mothers with young children. But all that was cold comfort. Whatever the echoes in our neighborhood, the raid was seared into my memory—and God knows what Stefan would be experiencing when he woke up. That is, if he was sleeping at all. I did not want to check. One more sign of my cowardice.

The evening's grotesque events continued to parade past me over and over as grimly as Richard III's murder victims haunting him before his final battle. Even with Marco curled up next to me, nestled into my armpit as he often did at night upstairs in bed, I felt completely at sea. How was I supposed to live the rest of my life after this cataclysm, how was I even supposed to get through tomorrow? I hadn't been the one taken off to jail, and yet I felt as trapped as if it *had* been me.

Police had polluted my home, treated me and Stefan like criminals or worse, insulted me, degraded us both. I could never recover the man I'd been minutes before it all happened: blithely unaware that disaster was about to tear apart my assumptions that life was solid and safe. I'd grown up in New York City but had never been mugged, never even *seen* a crime, and I confess that despite having encountered murder in Michiganapolis, the past six years of peace had been more than a balm, they were a narcotic. Thanks to Stefan's amazing memoir and my getting tenure, we had more money than we could have hoped for. And that was even with Stefan tithing a portion of his royalties to the church he had joined.

But what did money matter?

Marco stirred against me, the underside of his muzzle very warm, and it was as if someone had nudged me and asked, "Are you kidding?" He was right. Money meant we could pay Vanessa whatever it would take to clear our names if we had to. The law had been turned against us tonight in one way—who knew what could happen next? Money meant we weren't completely defenseless—or so I hoped.

Marco sighed in his sleep and rolled over on his back, looking adorable. Where had he hidden himself during the raid? I wish I could have had the sense (or courage?) to join him.

I must have slept, because Marco was nosing my cheek the way he does when I haven't gotten up early enough for him. He'd been woken up by the rising sun and the birdsong outside.

I stumbled to the back door to let him out into the fenced yard and pee, standing further back than I usually did, as if to keep anyone from seeing me. There was still coffee left, and after putting out Marco's kibble, I contentedly watched him munch away. He wasn't a gobbler like some dogs, and seemed almost catlike in the way he took his meals. Despite everything that had happened, I felt myself grinning with enjoyment watching him. And then I remembered Vanessa telling me the local cops shot dogs during raids. Yesterday's horrors rushed back in like some kind of alien horde in a sci-fi movie.

That was it. I couldn't even try to rest a bit more.

I heard Stefan padding downstairs and heading into the kitchen. Marco trotted up to him, but when he was ignored, he settled down on his dog bed and lay there licking his chops, looking contented. If only I had his gift for letting go so easily!

Stefan was wearing the blue velvet vintage smoking jacket and silk pajamas I'd gotten him partly as a joke when his book hit the *New York Times* best-seller list. They matched his eyes, but today made him look like an exiled monarch who'd seen his palace go up in flames. He didn't answer my "Good morning," just moved around the kitchen listlessly, picking up a *Vanity Fair*, moving a fruit bowl, fiddling with things as if trying to remember what their purpose was or what one even did in this room. It was a crazy comparison, but I thought of Mary Tyrone in *Long Day's Journey into Night*, high on morphine, lost to the world and lost in herself. Stefan and I had seen it twice at the Stratford Festival in Ontario, with an amazing actress playing Mary. Each time, we had sat long after the theater emptied out, too stunned to move. Mary's last line in that play was "And I was happy—for a time." Was that our fate? Had we been happy for a time, and now the darkness would always surround us?

"Are you cold?" I asked him fatuously.

Stefan nodded, but he didn't look at me.

"Why don't you sit down, I'll make breakfast."

"Not hungry," he murmured. Well, I wasn't either. But I seemed doomed to say stupid things.

"Coffee?"

He shrugged an okay, and I brought him coffee, but he still wouldn't sit down.

I waited for him to say something, but when he was silent for an unbearable ten minutes, I had to speak: "Will you tell me what happened last night?"

Now he sat at the glass-topped table, put his mug down carefully, and just began without even clearing his throat. "They called me faggot and I don't know what else. After I was out on the lawn, with somebody's boot on my ass, they dragged me into that truck or tank or whatever it was."

"It's an armored personnel carrier."

"Whatever. It felt like a tank. One of them was in front of me and one of them was behind me. Inside, there were bench seats facing each other. It was like being in Iraq or something like that, and I was the roadside bomber they had caught and were going to execute. I kept waiting for them to pull over and dump me in a ditch." He gulped and went on. "I was handcuffed to one of the benches and I heard the cops—they were cops, right?—I heard one of them talking to somebody, and when I looked up, I could see him entering information on—on some kind of dashboard computer. Maybe it was a tablet. I'm not sure."

He breathed in deeply, face creased in pain.

"My picture was up there, my driver's license maybe? It was really cold in there. We kept driving and then pulled up somewhere, a metal door opened, very loud, and when they took me out, it was some kind of garage, I think. The same guys took me into a tiny room and sat me down. It was sterile, the fluorescent lights were blinking a little and I could see that even with my eyes shut. They left me there for hours, I think." He swallowed hard a few times. "I felt like I'd never get out."

I was tempted to stop him, because the recital was filling me with despair and terror. I imagined myself there with him and it was horrible. Vanessa's injunction came back: "Let him talk."

Stefan went on without any prompting. "I didn't know if you were okay or not. What if you were dead, or injured? And I thought Marco might have run away with the front door open."

I winced—how come he had worried about our puppy and I hadn't?

"I didn't know what was going on, Nick, why I was there, and what they wanted, they never said. All I kept thinking was that I wished I had a gun."

"What?"

For the first time that morning, his eyes met mine and he looked crazed, possessed, like a warrior leading troops into a hopeless battle.

"You wanted a *gun?*" I asked.

"Oh, yeah. I would have shot every motherfucker in sight."

Stefan's an introvert, gets angry only rarely, and when he does, it can be explosive. But I'd never heard him like this. He was almost growling. In that moment, I realized not having bought a gun a few years ago might have been one of the wisest decisions of my life.

"Did they hurt you?" I managed to ask.

He grimaced. "You mean did they put electrodes on my balls or waterboard me? No. But I was strip-searched."

"You were—?"

He nodded and looked away. "All I had on was pajama pants. But they took them off anyway and they made me bend over, and they lifted my—" He squeezed his eyes shut. "They lifted my balls and looked underneath. I won't tell you what they said. I'll never tell anyone what they said. But if I could kill them right now, I would, and I'd die happy. Every single one of them, a bullet to the brain."

I wanted to say something to talk him down from the ledge he was on, but I knew Vanessa was right in urging me to just shut up and listen.

"They strip-searched me," he said again, coldly, as if observing the scene from a tremendous distance. And then he shrugged, helplessly. I felt his silence now was an invitation.

Picturing what had happened to Stefan, I felt bombarded by every scene of police brutality I'd ever watched on TV or in the movies. "How many of them?" I asked.

He squinted. "At least two. They kept poking me with a gun or a baton or something and—" He shook his head. "I can't believe this is happening to me. In *Michiganapolis.*"

Stefan's parents were Holocaust survivors who'd hidden their Jewishness and pretended to be Catholic when he was growing up, then revealed that he was actually Jewish when he was a teenager. I wasn't really sure how much they'd told him about their war years when the secret was finally out, but I was certain the unspoken trauma they'd passed on to him in all the years before that had just been re-triggered by the SWAT team. I despise the American habit of comparing everyone you

22

don't like to Nazis, but it was impossible to escape thinking like that this morning.

The doorbell rang and Stefan jerked back in his chair as if he'd been punched in the chest. I froze, but Marco woke up and trotted off to see who was there and I had to follow. "It can't be them, it can't be them," I kept repeating softly as I made my way into the foyer, ready to grab Marco if there was trouble.

I didn't have to.

Vanessa bounded in, looking even more glamorous than yesterday, this time in an orange and black checkered pants suit and ropes of amber beads around her neck. "I brought you donuts," she said. "Tim Horton's. Even if you're not hungry, these are no ordinary donuts."

I followed her into the kitchen where she greeted Stefan as casually as if she'd been invited. She set her iPhone down on the island and quickly found a plate for the donuts, set them out on the table. Stefan actually took one. I guess nobody ever said no to Vanessa. Marco certainly liked her. Or the donuts. He sat there glancing from one to the other.

"You look amazing," I heard myself saying. It was inappropriate, but I was punch drunk, I suppose. "Do you ever sleep?"

"Me? Never. *Kidding!* Of course I sleep. When I need to. I also swim, stay hydrated, and my sister is a model, so I know makeup secrets of the gods."

She whirled around to Stefan. "You guys have to stick together now. What happened last night can drive any couple apart." She cocked her head. "Tragedy does that to people. I've seen it too often, especially when the cops are involved."

"I want to sue those bastards," I said.

She smiled. "For what? Protecting the Homeland? Are you unpatriotic or something?"

"What are you talking about?"

"My guess is that they would end up claiming the whole thing was connected to national security. That's the best way out of a tight corner—it trumps everything and they can say or do whatever they want to. Don't you know what kind of country we live in now? Stefan could have wound up in some secret base abroad if somebody had pushed the right buttons."

"You mean there's nothing we can do about it?"

"Nope. He wasn't hurt, and the damage to your property is minimal, I assume?"

"There wasn't any."

"That's it, then. I've seen houses that were torn apart, every damned dish and vase and glass and picture frame and ashtray broken, paper files shredded, beds and chairs and couches ripped open. I told you before, you're lucky." Then she added, "And Stefan was released quickly. If the DEA had been involved, they could have held him for days without food or water. Not on purpose. By accident. They sometimes forget they have suspects."

I didn't even want to imagine that. "But isn't there some way to find out how this mess started?"

"I told you, I have contacts on the force. I'm asking some questions, maybe I'll come up with something, but don't hold your breath, guys."

Stefan was silent through all of our conversation. He'd broken a donut into pieces on the table and was eating them one at a time, carefully.

"You're a sleuth, aren't you?" Vanessa asked, folding her arms and looking a little stern.

"No, I'm a professor. I'm a bibliographer."

"Bullshit. I know who you are. I know you've solved some murders in the past. Get out your gear and start sleuthing."

"And when we find who did it?" Stefan said. "I will kill him."

Vanessa turned, planted both hands on the table and leaned into his face. "No way, José." Casual phrase, tough attitude: She could have been Maggie Thatcher declaring war on Argentina. "You will *want* to kill whoever set you up. I don't blame you. I'd feel the same way. But you are *not* going to do it. I've defended guilty clients and defended innocent ones and I much prefer the ones who don't keep me up at night, worrying about what kind of person I am."

4

Stefan had actually begun to munch on a second donut when Vanessa said, "I need to warn you about something."

I started laughing. She and Stefan both gawked at me as if they were afraid I was succumbing to hysteria.

"I'm sorry," I sputtered. "That just made me think of that movie— you know which one!— where Isabella Rossellini gives people a potion for eternal youth and then right after they drink it, she says, 'And now, a warning.'"

They both looked blank, but I kept going, even though I couldn't remember the movie's name. "And I think Meryl Streep or someone like that shouts '*Now* a warning?'"

No recognition whatsoever from either of them, so I backtracked and prompted Vanessa: "Okay, what do you want to warn us about?"

She sat down at the table, which I took to be a bad sign. Crossing her long legs, she said, "Well, you were lucky that the raid took place at night, because it apparently didn't get into the paper—I checked—but it could show up tomorrow. And there's a good chance it'll be on local TV news tonight. So you could be facing a media shit storm. Whatever you do, do *not* talk to any reporters. Check your caller ID, and just smile and keep going if you're out at the mall or wherever and someone tries to ask you questions. Don't even say 'No comment.' That sounds guilty."

"But we're *not* guilty," Stefan muttered. "We haven't done anything. We're victims."

Vanessa sighed. "It's a juicy story. I could write it myself."

Me too. So many sensationalistic angles. Start with us being a gay couple—for some people that was story enough. Or faculty members suspected of nefarious activities. Then there was "Prominent Writer—Does He Have a Secret Life?" Or "College Town Scene of Raid." And "Terrorists in the Midwest?" On and on and on.

Stefan surprisingly kept munching on his donut, but I couldn't imagine eating anything right then. Marco edged closer to the table, gazing up at Stefan's hand as intently as if he were willing a piece of the donut to fall to the floor. He wagged his tail a few times hopefully, even though we did not feed him table scraps.

"Will it blow over?" I asked Vanesa.

"Possibly," she said.

The landline rang over by the Sub-Zero refrigerator, and we all stared at it. Even Marco. I got up and grabbed it because I was closest, and brought the receiver reluctantly to my ear.

"Hello?"

"This is Dean Bullerschmidt. I want to see both of you in my office in one hour." He hung up. Typical. He hadn't even asked—or cared—which one of us had answered. The dean was what my mother would have called "an ugly customer." Pig-eyed and pig-headed, as fat as New Jersey's Chris Christie, he had barely half that governor's charm. He was power-mad, had never risen to provost or president, and exacted revenge for this failure on the faculty who crossed him in any way, real or imaginary. He'd been known to drive even male professors from his office in tears.

"Bullerschmidt wants to see us," I told Stefan.

"Fuck."

Vanessa raised an eyebrow and I explained who he was, and why we dreaded even random encounters with him. She frowned and then seemed to work it out: "Sounds like someone on the inside—a cop, I mean—contacted this dean of yours to make trouble for you, or how else would he know so soon? Boys, you must really have pissed somebody off, big-time."

Her iPhone chirped, she jumped up to check the number, let the call go to voicemail, thumbed a quick text and said, "Gotta go. This could be a lead."

I followed her to the door and thanked her again for last night, for rescuing us.

"I did what I always do," she said nonchalantly. "First rule, defuse the situation and let them know they can't steamroll you. I mean all of us. The cops, the prosecutors, and lots of judges hate defense attorneys more than they hate criminals and suspects. They think what we do is immoral—they think we're worse than the bad guys. I stood up for you, but I also stood up for the criminal justice system, which they keep trying to smash."

When I let her out, I was wary about returning to the kitchen. What was I supposed to say? How were Stefan and I supposed to conduct our everyday lives from now on? I'd never been through anything this traumatic, but Marco came trotting up to me, and I realized he would be part of the solution. Whatever had happened, he still needed to be fed, walked, let out into the yard, groomed, cared for, loved. There was no reason for him to suffer in any way because we had. Maybe the quotidian would be the light at the end of this miserable tunnel.

I picked him up and carried him into the kitchen, and sat by Stefan. Marco poked his snout in the direction of the donuts, snuffling in every stray molecule he could.

"We should get dressed," Stefan observed. He looked funereal.

We cleaned up, showered and put on academic drag: blazers and ties. We gave Marco his command: "Time to guard the house," and he trooped off into the living room to curl up in his dog bed near the fireplace.

"I'll drive," I said. Getting into my Lexus, I didn't just feel like a schoolboy called to the principal's office, but like a felon. And if I could have somehow driven out of our garage invisibly, I would have. As we pulled down the driveway and onto our quiet suburban-looking street, a sense of exposure and shame constricted my breathing so sharply that Stefan reached over, grabbed my arm and said, "It'll be okay. What can he do to us?" I think he meant compared to what had already happened.

I drove off, saying, "He can make us feel like mice he's going to feed to his snake, *that's* what he can do." Bullerschmidt excelled at intimidation; in that, he was a perfect administrator at a university top-heavy with these arbiters of policy who earned lavish six-figure salaries. The university was supposed to be a seat of learning and a place for collegiality, but it had become something very different during Michigan's hard times. It was now more like an empire, ruled by despots who doled out favors here or there, and were more interested in prestige and fundraising than education. As for faculty, we were meant to keep quiet no matter what outrage we saw committed.

SUM's six-thousand-acre campus is amazingly green and gorgeous in spring and summer, but none of that touched me as we drove to the faculty parking lot closest to the dean's office. He was housed in one of the oldest buildings: appropriately enough, a granite and sandstone Gothic Revival mini-castle bristling with turrets. But thanks to the current campus craze for remodeling, his office suite on the top floor was weirdly contemporary. It looked more like a high-tech kitchen than anything else: everything was white marble or brushed stainless steel. There was a plaque indicating which alumni had financed the extreme makeover, but I didn't bother reading it on the way in. This was all part of an effort across campus to have offices and buildings subsidized by donations, since state funding had collapsed as part of the overall budget. Anything could be branded now by anyone, as long as their check cleared.

Things were so bad that if the administration could have sold SUM to China, the sale would have gone through. They could even have kept the same initials, SUM, and just made it Sino University of Michigan.

Bullerschmidt's secretary, Mrs. Inkpen, generally neutral in clothes and attitude, didn't even look up at us from her brushed steel desk, as if we were tainted. Her attitude was as frigid as the air conditioning kept the office.

Without shifting her glance from her Apple laptop, she said quietly, "Go on in, gentlemen." We did.

Bullerschmidt had set his desk in front of a windowless wall and so there was no way you could be distracted by a view behind him. His stare was equal parts Medusa and Anthony Hopkins in *The Silence of the Lambs*, and he did not invite us to sit down. He tore into us immediately: "If you have any consideration for this institution at all, I would like you two to consider a leave of absence next semester. Paid, of course."

This was unheard of—we'd just spent the year on sabbatical.

"Why?" I asked, glad there hadn't been any attempt to lull us before the assault.

"It's obvious," he rumbled. "Your presence on campus would be a distraction. We have never had faculty disgraced in this manner."

"I'd say it's the police who disgraced themselves. We haven't been charged with anything and whatever report they got that sent them to our house was obviously phony."

Vanessa was right, I thought: someone clearly had it in for us. And that scared me because whoever it was had to be both malign and clever: setting a SWAT team in motion and creating separate hassles for us at the university. What other trouble could they foment?

I pressed him. "The whole raid was bogus—someone reported a hostage at our house. Pure bullshit. Or didn't your source on the inside tell you that?"

He didn't reply, and I said, "No, probably not. I think somebody is playing you for a fool, Dean Bullerschmidt."

He flushed deep red from neck to forehead like some kind of chameleon instantaneously changing its color; it was alarming and grotesque.

"We cannot allow faculty to behave this way," he rumbled.

"You mean be victimized? That's nothing new around here." I had never spoken to an administrator like this before, but then I'd never been manhandled by cops, either. I was mad as hell and I wasn't going to take it anymore.

"Admit it," I said. "You're just worried about bad PR." Universities loathe negative press as much as slugs hate salt.

Bullerschmidt did not concede the point. He just waited. But he'd picked the wrong tactic. Stefan was still so shell-shocked his normal responses weren't operating. Besides, he was introverted at the best of times, so he couldn't be bullied by silence. And me, I was enraged by what had happened, and that was quickly burning through my shame the way men in old French novels squander their inheritances on horses and whores.

So I didn't just wait. I grinned. Evilly, I hope. And then I spoke up as curtly as I could muster, "If that's all you had to say to us, an email or a text message would have wasted much less time." I tapped Stefan's shoulder and we turned to leave. At the door, I added, "We haven't done anything wrong, and we're not taking a leave."

It wasn't as memorable as Douglas MacArthur's "I shall return" in World War II, but it seemed to rally Stefan, who looked at me with something less than zombie indifference. Bullerschmidt wasn't letting go just yet, though.

"There's something else we have to discuss," he said darkly. "That *book*." He made it sound like something loathsome, and both of us knew he meant Stefan's work-in-progress.

A year ago, Stefan had caught a student of his, Casey Silver, committing plagiarism on one of his papers. It was grossly obvious: a steal of several paragraphs from an essay in *The New Yorker*; how could he have thought Stefan would miss it? He asked Casey to rewrite it, which was a very generous response, because most professors would have just given the kid a zero on the paper or even flunked him for the whole course. Stefan thought asking for a rewrite would resolve the situation, but it didn't, or not in the way he expected. It turned out that Casey had suffered extreme bullying in high school, and being confronted even mildly about plagiarism had apparently triggered a cataclysmic shame spiral. The poor boy hanged himself. In Parker Hall, no less. From an exposed pipe running across the ceiling in the building's lobby.

Stefan felt responsible, though I tried as hard as I could to convince him he couldn't have known it would happen. His sabbatical had been coming up and instead of traveling, he decided to stay home and cope with his trauma by doing what he did best: writing a book. When it was still only a partial draft, his new agent quickly got him a contract for *Fieldwork in the Land of Grief* (which Stefan and I usually referred to as *Fieldwork*). Bullying, after all, was a hot topic. Signing the big-bucks contract made the local news and enraged Casey's family who lobbied the administration to put the kibosh on Stefan's project. Their pressure pushed SUM's president and provost both to personally appeal to Stefan to give it up, but he refused.

"You cannot keep writing that book," the dean rumbled now as if trying to sound as magisterial as Winston Churchill. "You cannot *publish* that book. It's offensive."

Stefan stepped forward, fully present now, chin up. "If I drop this project, I will never understand what happened and what it means."

"You're putting your personal feelings ahead of the family of that unfortunate young man, and ahead of the reputation of this noble university." Wow, I thought, that sounded like something the dean had practiced for a press release or an interview.

"Maybe. Maybe not," Stefan said. "But you can't censor faculty members and tell us what kind of books we can write."

Bullerschmidt nodded sourly as if he'd imagined Stefan using just those words. "I will not be held responsible for the consequences of your recklessness," he said. "Remember that. Whatever happens, I warned you. We've *all* warned you."

I was stunned by this exchange, and grabbed Stefan's arm to pull him out of there. But before we left, the dean stood, picked up a tooled-leather wastepaper basket and spit heavily into it. *That's* what he thought of us.

On the way to our car, Stefan was muttering to himself, but I didn't ask him to speak up. Driving home, I started to fulminate. "He's a dictator!"

Stefan kept his thoughts to himself, and I wondered if he'd been intimidated by the dean. I knew that *Fieldwork* wasn't all that far along; maybe giving it up wouldn't be a major sacrifice, but how could I be sure? Stefan always showed me his books while he worked on them, but he'd been keeping this one so private it felt like he was either ashamed of it or he was afraid I wouldn't like it, which seemed peculiar.

"Have you ever thought that writing this book might be a mistake?" I asked.

"You're taking the dean's side?" he snapped.

"No, nothing like that. It's just . . ." I hesitated. "Is it right to profit from someone's suffering?"

Stefan shook his head defiantly. "It's my book. I have to write it."

I couldn't argue with that. He was a writer, I was only a bibliographer.

Traffic back from campus was nonexistent, since the tens of thousands of students were gone now that classes had ended, and we were home in less than five minutes. I was fired up now by more than just the coffee I'd been drinking for hours. I was outraged. We loosened our ties, took off our jackets, let Marco out in the backyard and sat in the gazebo watching him chase squirrels. We'd had the yard redone when Stefan's memoir started selling like crazy and now it was much more private and lush. The oaks and maples had an understory of hemlocks and purple or white azaleas along the back fence, and we'd planted wildly fragrant viburnums along the sides of the yard.

I was relieved to see that Stefan's color was starting to return and he seemed much less withdrawn. It probably helped being outdoors and being safe at home.

Safe? How safe were we really now? I wasn't paranoid. Someone, somewhere was plotting against us. I didn't say any of this aloud, I didn't want to spoil the moment, because Stefan was more present each minute he sat there. I was sure that Bullerschmidt's high-handedness had penetrated his fog, and maybe my speechifying had, too.

"You know, there's nothing he can do to us," I said fiercely. "We have tenure and they can only take it away and fire us for things like moral turpitude, or intellectual dishonesty. Having a SWAT team as house guests doesn't fit either of those categories."

Stefan almost smiled. "I can't believe he accused us of not caring about SUM." He shook his head. "Twice, really. Well, me twice and you once."

"It was slimy. But he'd say anything to dump us, or dump the problem he thinks we represent."

Stefan frowned as if he didn't quite follow, and I'm not entirely sure I knew what I meant, but that was okay. He surprised me by saying, "Maybe we should have some lunch. We can't just keep eating donuts. I can't, anyway."

I checked my watch and it was close to noon. "Let me take Marco for a short walk before we have lunch." I went into the garage to get the leash, shovel, and plastic bag ready, then rounded up Marco and headed out, feeling oddly braver for having stood up to the dean. And somehow, being with Marco seemed so completely normal as we made our way to the small neighborhood park a few blocks off that I didn't feel as self-conscious as I'd thought I would.

I was about to cross at the corner where there was a stop sign, when a car screeched to a stop only a few feet from us. I jerked Marco back from the road, almost falling as I did so. He yelped at being pulled so sharply and I crouched down to comfort him. That's when I heard a car window glide down and the driver say, "Walk faster, or next time, I'll hit you."

He sped off so quickly that I wasn't able to get his license plate or focus well on the car. I hadn't seen his face, but I registered the menace in his voice.

This was no joke. And I was frozen. Those squealing brakes were like a broken neon sign, flashing erratically in my head.

Less than twelve hours after the raid, I was once again terrified for my life. He could have run me and Marco over. I've never fainted in my life before, but I came very close to it right then. I forced myself to keep walking, made it to the little neighborhood park planted with enormous weeping willows, sat down on one of the benches, with Marco at my feet. I was stunned by what had just happened, and by knowing I would have to tell Stefan.

5

Even in my renewed state of shock, the small park of just about two acres worked on me like a massage, easing the tension out of my body, clearing my mind. A light breeze made the willow fronds sway as languidly as if they were underwater plants. On his retractable leash, Marco wandered and sniffed just as much as I'd let him. This was always a quiet spot because it had been donated to the city years ago by a local real estate millionaire, with the specification that it never have any slides, swings, jungle gym, sandbox or anything like that. Surrounded by an elaborate cast iron black fence, and with only one entrance, it was meant to be a place of contemplation, not a playground. Teens didn't loiter there at night because it was "boring," and if people did bring their children during the day, they were usually in strollers and were wheeled away as quickly as possible if they started to fuss or cry.

The little park had never felt so much like a refuge before. Sitting there alone, I thought that this was the kind of time when people say "What next, what could possibly happen next?" and someone superstitious tells them to be quiet. But I couldn't shush myself. I *did* wonder what else Fate had in store for me after my last handful of years of quiet achievement and contentment. Was my luck changing back again?

I had entered a department of misfits, malcontents, and misanthropes under a cloud: I was a "spousal hire." That means that EAR had wanted to hire Stefan, not me, and had to scramble to create a position for me to make sure Stefan accepted SUM's offer. As is usually the case, the circumstances were held against me in a group of professional divas and detractors. Not that the department needed any more reasons to dislike me, or even the idea of me. I wasn't respected for having authored a secondary bibliography of Edith Wharton, despite all the work that went into the five-year project. I'd read everything ever written about

Wharton—whether books, articles, or reviews—and summarized it so that students and scholars had all of Wharton scholarship for over a century laid out for them in one fat book. If I'd have written anything that used the latest impenetrable critical jargon, something that might sell only a handful of copies, I would have been considered at least up-to-date by my colleagues. But my book was too practical a work, too useful; bibliographies were as unglamorous and old-fashioned to most academics as spittoons.

My cousin Sharon worked at Columbia University as a research librarian, and she'd once quipped, "If Tolstoy had been a professor, he would have said that every unhappy department is unhappy in its own way." The Department of English, American Studies, and Rhetoric owed its sniping and bitterness to a history of division: The faculty teaching rhetoric (basic composition) had been forced on English and American Studies when the Department of Rhetoric was dissolved in a budget-cutting move. Nobody wanted the Rhetoric refugees, who were considered second-class academics and treated like smelly drunken guests at a wedding. Force people to work together, share a building, serve on committees, and you end up with volcanic animosities building up pressure year after year.

And I was soon derided, even suspected, because I truly enjoyed teaching basic writing well before I ever taught literature classes like an Edith Wharton seminar and The American Crime Novel. Teaching writing skills demanded tremendous dedication and time, and most faculty preferred to be as untrammeled as possible. To them, tenured positions meant freedom to spend as many hours away from campus and their students as possible. But there was more working against me: once I'd gotten drawn into murder investigations, I had become a cross between a pariah and a joke.

Then the bequest by my former student had totally sealed my fate. The small fortune he left to the department had severe restrictions on it: the money would go to inviting an author to teach and speak there once a year; I was to be in charge of this new lecture series; and it wasn't named after the student, but after me. More surprisingly, the money would pass to a leukemia charity if I either died or left the university. If EAR wanted the money, they had to accept my rise in status, and my new-found independence from Stefan, and even the rest of the department.

I suddenly had my own little bailiwick: The Nick Hoffman Fellowship. No, it was more than that, it was an oasis in a desert of academic insanity.

If I'd been disliked before, now I was hated. Despite that, I was courted, because of course everyone had their favorite candidate for the yearly visitor, given that the stipend was $25,000 and the work wasn't onerous. Fellows had to give a lecture, a reading, teach some workshops, and remain in residence for only one month. So I was sought after even by people who felt it was demeaning to try to win me over. They resented my new importance, and that I'd been given promotion to full professor by the dean (though it was only because of the fellowship and the university wanting me to look better on paper). I even had my own administrative assistant to run the little program, and a larger office than before. Hell, larger wasn't as important to me as being out of Parker Hall's basement, which I'd been exiled to years ago.

The fact that I had any real office was the coup de grace for my enemies. A new initiative at the university was dedicated to making all the departments more "open," and in ours, that had translated into two floors of Parker being gutted and remodeled last summer, right before Stefan and I took our sabbaticals together. Some of what they had done was practical: every individual office had a fire extinguisher because the building was so old and had long been considered a fire trap. But that was the most positive change. Other renovations were insidious, though on the brighter side, it didn't look as much like the setting for a slasher film as before.

Why the changes in our building? Because at SUM, appearances were what counted, not realities. The university was constantly reinventing itself rhetorically, coming up with new slogans like "We Care"— seriously! These were always the result of endless deliberations in specially constituted committees with impressive-sounding names, and later were rolled out through a new mission statement. It was pomposity masquerading as thoughtfulness, and typically meant about as much as the campaign buttons of the losing party the day after a national election.

Universities were not just political in their infighting, but also worked in similarly hierarchical ways that bred resentment. And people were jealous to the point of mild hysteria about their perks, so the redesign of EAR's two floors hit the department like the barbarians sacking

Rome. Except for the administrators who were in their own suite, Stefan as writer-in-residence, and little old me and my administrative assistant, everyone else now had the cubicles for office space that you might find in a call center in India. Bathrooms, meeting rooms, the supply room, mail room, and copy room were one floor down along with more cubicles for graduate assistants and temporary faculty. Full-timers seeking privacy or relief from the din in the department sometimes lurked down there like unpopular kids at a birthday party, since they were less likely to be found. Or they just stayed away entirely.

So, picture the main floor of the department as an enormous large rectangle. Three actual offices with doors had been carved out on the short sides, each office about ten feet by twenty feet. Not palatial, but the old fifteen-foot ceilings and enormous windows made them seem bigger than they were. And the architects had kept some original, heavy oak doors that were twelve feet high and had old-fashioned transoms. On the north end the chair and the associate chair had their offices, with one between them shared by their secretaries, and all three of those offices were connected.

The elevator was in the middle of the long, eastern side of the building with staircases flanking it. I avoided the stairs because they were very old and the metal treads echoed abominably, as if you were in a hellish high school.

My office was all the way across the building on the south end, and it was connected with my assistant's. Stefan's office was on the other side of hers, but without a connecting door to hers. Between these triads was a yawning space studded with four groups of six cubicles; each group separated by what I guess you'd call a corridor four or five feet wide. The partitions separating faculty were only four feet high and privacy was nonexistent. In the actual offices, the high ceilings made for a feeling of openness, whereas here in what some people called "The Pit," they turned everything sterile. Even worse, the windows facing the Pit had been redone, and now had electronic blinds which were light-sensitive and adjusted themselves or closed on their own schedule. Nobody on-site could control them.

The set-up was a shock the first time I saw it, and the shock hadn't faded much over the course of my sabbatical year. I suppose it could have been worse, and there could have just been rows of desks and chairs like some old-time typing pool. One floor down, the only rooms with doors were for supplies, the photocopier, and the mailroom directly under my side of the building, and meeting rooms directly opposite. The rest of that floor was also set up entirely as open space with cubicles, mingling graduate assistants and temporary faculty. Temporary, of course, is an odd term to use for people who keep getting hired every year—but that's the way of a university. Never call things what they really are.

The surprising architectural changes in Parker Hall had been made over a summer, the university's typical policy when doing anything unpopular or possibly controversial. The student newspaper was published infrequently, people weren't around, and it was the best time to be sneaky. Returning faculty had been stunned. The offices of the Department of EAR, which had been stuck in the early nineteenth century, now looked painfully up-to-date: an anonymous business staffed by drones who couldn't talk behind people's backs anymore because the acoustics allowed even whispers to carry many partitions away.

My own office was nothing extraordinary, but it was of course a real office, not a cubicle, and spacious enough. People have killed for less, though, and in a department that was all knives and very little steak, I was now an even easier target than I'd ever been. Colleagues congratulated me, but it was fake. They thought I didn't deserve the step up (or the view), and they hoped I'd fail or bring scandal upon myself in some way that would invalidate the gift and get me ousted somehow. If the department were a movie, I would have been the guy holed up in a boarded-up house surrounded by flesh-eating ghouls.

I even sensed resentment from the new chair, a former friend, Juno Dromgoole. Once foul-mouthed and excessive, a stormy cross between Bette Midler and Tina Turner who dressed with excessive panache, the professor of Canadian Studies had toned herself way down. She was still as haughty as ever, but now with the aloof distance of a dowager empress. Juno had liked and teased me before, but now she seemed to suspect me. Of what? Wanting her job?

It was a very strange reorganization in a department that had long felt under siege. Stefan and I had been teaching there for over fifteen years and had seen the department shrink as class sizes went up. When senior professors retired, their positions weren't filled, but temporary professors—adjuncts—were hired to teach their courses at a quarter of the cost. Fiction writing classes that once had fifteen students went to twenty, then twenty-five, and now were at thirty on the way to thirty-five. Stefan said you couldn't possibly teach writing well with a class that big, but there was nothing he could do about it. SUM wanted fewer full-time faculty everywhere and "efficiency" in departments that weren't bringing in outside funding through grants. Read: do more with less.

Marco was nuzzling my leg, which meant he was done with my contemplation, so I headed home with him, reluctantly, looking around me for anything suspicious all the way back home. And when I could see our house a block away, it felt painfully exposed somehow, as if this time the SWAT team was about to descend on ropes from helicopters. The image was so fiercely real, it could have been a hallucination, and for a moment I had an urge to turn and run.

I didn't need to force myself to keep going, though, because Marco was pulling me home. The last thing I expected when I approached our driveway was laughter, but I could hear it funneling out from the kitchen window, and I knew we had a visitor, because there was only one person who made Stefan laugh that hard: Father Ryan Burke.

I let myself in and Marco raced to the kitchen for water. Father Ryan was at the counter with a mug of coffee, out of his "clericals," in skinny jeans and a black polo shirt, and he beamed at me. Stefan must have called him while I was gone and he'd walked over from St. Jude, and I was glad Stefan had been forced by Bullerschmidt's call to get dressed, because it made the day seem slightly more normal. We had one neighbor who would amble down to his mailbox in his robe and slippers at all times of the day and I dreaded becoming as heedless of time and place as that.

"Nick, I'm very sorry about your trouble."

"Thanks, Father Ryan." He insisted on us just using his first name, even when he was wearing his collar, but I wasn't comfortable with that yet.

"It's shameful. Not my idea of America."

He was not my idea of a priest. Tall and slim, he had the dark eyes, curly black hair, angular jaw and high cheekbones of a Romantic poet.

Or my image of one, anyway. He was thirtyish, easy-going, and surprisingly progressive, with a resonant mellifluous voice you'd expect from a radio announcer. Stefan said his homilies were terrific, and I could believe that. Ryan was also a rock climber, a marksman, an avid hiker, and Stefan said that he brought those experiences into what he shared with his parishioners.

Father Ryan had guided Stefan through his long conversion process and had become a friend. At first I was jealous of the time they spent together, but gradually I saw how happy Stefan was to be converting, how deeply contented, and I let go. I grew grateful that Father Ryan had initially sought Stefan out with questions about publishing a book of his own and their conversations had unexpectedly led Stefan to start attending Mass, looking for a spiritual center in his life. His career at that point was a disaster, and he'd had enough dark nights of the soul to fill a calendar. As the mystics put it, he'd been "hollowed out" by suffering. And then one afternoon, at Mass, as Stefan described it, he knew that this was going to be his new home. "I felt it as sure as the blood was moving through my veins," he reported later.

We talked a bit now, Ryan encouraging us to take a vacation or do something that would heal the injury. "The summer's barely started. Do something, go somewhere. Take a cruise."

Stefan shook his head. "There isn't any scenery in the world that would make up for the raid and how they treated us."

Ryan nodded, taking it in the way a smart, warm-hearted therapist might, not offering any bromides. And I was glad he didn't quote any Fathers of the Church at me, or talk about loving one's enemy. I had gotten used to Stefan relying on him, on them calling each other "brother," on Stefan going to Mass more than once a week, but Stefan's Catholicism was still new enough for me to feel uneasy at times about his midlife conversion and everything that went with it. Hearing them talk about Christ or "God's love" made me uncomfortable, since I'd been raised Jewish, and Jesus and the New Testament had always been terra incognita for me.

I knew there was no danger of Stefan becoming an ideologue, since he didn't have the personality for it, but now that he was a Roman Catholic, I felt he was connected to some very crazy people—at least distantly. Like all the bishops who had tried to muzzle American nuns for speaking out on social issues like marriage equality. And even conservatives at the church he attended, who were stuck in some 1950s version of their religion and seemed uncomfortable with the new pope's openness.

Father Ryan checked his watch, got up to give Stefan a hug, said "Don't forget to call me," and headed for the front door with his typical loping, athletic stride. He and Stefan sometimes played racquetball, and he usually won. I followed him out, and before he left, Ryan said intensely, "I hope they nail the bastard who screwed you guys over." I laughed. His talking like a real person was something Stefan had been enjoying for a long time, but it always startled me. I also admired the way he listened, with an intensity that felt musical, as if he were the accompanist in a violin sonata. Even his silence was participation.

Stefan was looking less crushed when I returned to the kitchen.

"Call him about what?" I asked.

"Whatever."

He looked almost embarrassed, so I asked, "Did Ryan help?" I asked. Between us, I could use the priest's first name without discomfort.

"For sure. He's always good to talk to. He was telling me about someone at church who grew up in East Germany before the Wall came down, and how she'd had the secret police drag her father away. He never came back."

"And that made you laugh?"

"No, what was funny was jokes they used to tell in East Germany." Before I could ask him to repeat some, he said, "You know, Vanessa was right. We have to start thinking about who could be behind the raid, who hates us enough to set something like that in motion."

"Okay. Deal. Ready for lunch? We have some of that casserole left."

Marco knew the word "lunch" and so we had to get him his kibble first. Once Marco was fed, pottied, and napping, Stefan broke out some of our favorite Belgian beer, Duvel. I put the "gourmet" mac 'n' cheese (made with penne riggate and a carrot/orange puree) in the microwave. I set the table and put out a pad and pen for each of us as if we were lawyers or diplomats at a conference. The only thing missing was a bottle of Appolinaris or some other European water for each of us.

When we were eating and the beers were half-downed, I said, "Doesn't Duvel mean Devil in Flemish? That's appropriate. Only a fiend would send a SWAT team for no reason."

Stefan put down his fork. "No, it has to be a good reason. Somebody who really hates us, wants us to suffer, maybe even go to prison."

"Are you sure? Maybe they just wanted to humiliate us. Or you." Stefan turned red. "Or me," I added uncertainly, feeling extra hungry. I guess fear and dread can do that. We ate in silence for a while. "I guess that's a good enough reason if you're unbalanced," I said.

"Bullerschmidt," Stefan finally brought out, as if turning over winning cards in baccarat. "It's obvious. He would have had us arrested in his office if he had the power to do it. He's vicious and he hates us."

That was no hyperbole. It wasn't just that my involvement in crime had made SUM look bad to the general public, or that Stefan's new book had the administration furious. Stefan and I had once, in a very unproductive and ill-advised visit to his home, basically accused the dean of murdering a new faculty member. That had been almost a decade ago, but he was the kind of man who didn't just nurse a grudge, he moved it into a private clinic.

"And—" Stefan added slowly. "How did he know about the police raid so quickly? Even the way he talked to us, it felt planned, like a little speech he practiced. Didn't you think so? He wasn't shocked, or even startled."

I nodded.

"So . . . what if he didn't have an informant inside the police, what if *he's* the one who started it? I just can't figure out who his target was, you or me . . ."

"Stefan, if either one of us gets hurt, so does the other. We both suffer." I sipped some beer and thought the dean was a very likely candidate, and someone sadistic enough to wait, plan, and strike unexpectedly. "But if this thing blows up and there's bad publicity, it doesn't make SUM look good."

"He's a bully. He's the Mother of All Bullies. He wouldn't care. He's beyond caring. He's like somebody in a Greek tragedy who wants revenge no matter what."

It fit. We'd seen Bullerschmidt intimidate his wife and faculty members, and we'd been on the receiving end of his steamrolling more than once, even before that time we confronted him in his home with our half-formed questions that sounded like accusations.

I had been listing pros and cons of the dean as a suspect, but I put my pen down. "This cannot be happening to us. Everything was perfect. You finally had a best seller. I finally got promoted to full professor and I have my own little power base in the department, and now we're like conspiracy theorists. This whole thing is unhinged."

Stefan leaned forward. "Nick. It's not a theory. It's real. Our house being invaded, me being dragged off to jail, that was real, that was our life, not somebody else's, not a book or a thriller. That's our life now, whether you like it or not. And it could be like this for a long time, how can we assume otherwise?"

The landline rang and we both froze, neither one of us moving to answer the call. We let the recorded message come on, and then a grotesque, ominous, echoing voice—clearly the product of a digital voice changer—filled the kitchen: "*We're not done with you yet.*"

Marco started to howl.

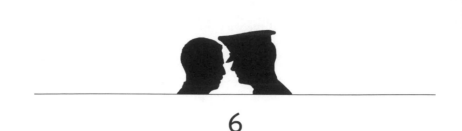

6

Stefan shushed Marco and looked at me, eyes bleak and angry. The call had been brief, but the sound of that voice was as dismal as the stench of burning plastic, and I felt my mouth go dry.

Marco headed out of the kitchen, possibly searching for someplace saner and quieter. It crossed my mind then to say to Stefan that we should quit our jobs, sell the house and move as far away from Michigan as possible. We'd have to downsize, but we'd be free of this insanity. From a golden routine, we had gone to base unpredictability.

Vanessa was right: we were privileged white men who had never been treated the way millions of less fortunate Americans were treated all the time. Academia made our lives even more remote from reality. It wasn't just a shock being manhandled and brutalized; it was as if we had been radically ripped from our own lives and dumped into an alternate reality.

"Son of a *bitch*," Stefan said, and it was the second time in an hour I'd heard him curse in a way he never did. I didn't object, but it bothered me that he didn't sound like himself.

"We need an unlisted number," I muttered, feeling a surge of helplessness, because I knew that nothing would make us safe, not even cancelling our landline. Nothing really could, not flight, not drugs. What was going to happen next? Hacking our email accounts? I thought of the terrible sad observation in Joan Didion's *Play It As It Lays*: "In the whole world there was not enough sedation as there was instantaneous peril."

Stefan rose and headed for the phone. "Hitting star fifty-seven gets you the number that called, right?"

"Forget it, Stefan. Knowing the number won't matter. Anybody taking the trouble to disguise their voice like that would make sure you couldn't track them. It's like murderers using gloves. Whoever called us would have used a burner phone, or a payphone if they could find one, or a soft phone."

Stefan sat back down heavily, pushed his plate away and finished his beer without any sign of enjoyment. "What the hell is a soft phone?"

"I don't know how it works exactly, but it's software so you can phone from your computer."

"But all of that can be traced somehow!"

"Only if you have a subpoena, or if you're the government and you don't need one."

"Great."

"Still think it's Bullerschmidt?"

Stefan frowned. "What do you mean?"

"He's malevolent, sure, but is he tech-savvy enough?" I answered my own question before Stefan could even consider it. "He wouldn't have to be, you can probably get one of those voice things on Amazon. And who knows what else."

"Or he hired someone."

I felt momentarily ashamed of myself at how ugly our speculation was. But then what we were saying about the dean wasn't uglier than what had happened to us.

"Couldn't *we* hire someone?" I asked.

"You mean a bodyguard?" Stefan squinted as if seeing an ex-Marine in a black Brioni suit standing in the corner of our kitchen.

"Maybe. I don't know. I'm not sure what I was thinking." I might have meant an assassin, but that never turned out well, in movies or in real life. Besides, we didn't have a definite target.

Stefan abruptly pushed back from the table and said, "Let's go out to the sunroom." He didn't even suggest cleaning up from our lunch, which was a sure sign he was distraught. Stefan wasn't obsessive-compulsive, but he was orderly, and leaving a mess behind was totally unlike him.

Marco was already there, curled up behind one of the well-stuffed bamboo-framed blue chairs and didn't even stir when we walked in and sat on the couch. I thought briefly of Vanessa's warning to talk outside, but I needed to be indoors, as little protection as that might be.

"I know I said I wanted to shoot people," Stefan brought out quietly. "But even if I did, it wouldn't change anything, it wouldn't help. There's no such thing as closure after last night."

"Well, maybe there's justice. Or revenge."

"The country's changed. Vanessa's right. Since the raid, I've been reading online about SWAT teams, and they've taken over the country. They're supposed to suppress violence, but they only end up causing more of it."

We had talked before about how too many Americans had lost their minds after 9/11 and the country had drifted closer and closer to being a national security state. How the president was somehow always referred to as the country's commander-in-chief even though he was constitutionally only that for the armed forces. How military men and woman and military equipment were used as background for photo ops and speeches.

I asked, "What do you mean they *cause* violence?"

He shook his head wearily. "The team shows up, regular people freak out, think they're being attacked by thieves. They're asleep, they're surprised, they don't hear anyone say the word 'police,' they panic. And even drug dealers can think they're being hit by other drug dealers. If anyone has a gun, they'll go for it, and sometimes use it. Either way, they're the ones who get shot, most of the time. Cops even use SWAT teams for things like insurance fraud. Some dermatologist cheating Medicare had a small army take him down."

"Wait—that actually happened?"

"Yes, he was in Memphis, but they had enough weapons for Mogadishu, and he was shot and killed. Nick, it's worse than what Vanessa told us. The War on Drugs, it's turned into the War on Terrorism—right here, right now. What I've been reading makes me sick, because it's become run-of-the-mill and only makes the news when there's a lawsuit or somebody important gets targeted by mistake. The standard for evidence to get a warrant now is unbelievably low, warrants are sealed a lot of the time, and cops don't get prosecuted if they shoot someone, but judges hammer you if you shoot a cop thinking your house is being invaded. The Fourth Amendment is basically dead."

Stefan was not given to rants, so a speech like this from him was unprecedented. Listening to these harsh realities was doubly unpalatable in a lovely, calm, blue and gold room filled with philodendrons whose leaves were heart-shaped.

"You haven't been checking out any *crazy* websites, have you?" I had to ask. I didn't know what being humiliated in jail might have driven him to. I could see him diving into survivalist or libertarian forums, going over the edge after he'd been so profoundly abused. It *was* abuse to turn shock and awe tactics on an American citizen with no criminal record. SUM's writer-in-residence, for God's sake, a *professor*.

"Everything I read was legit, not rumors or conspiracy theory. Like the *Los Angeles Times. The Denver Post. The New York Times.* This isn't made up, Nick. It's *news*. It's *real*. Judges sometimes even give the cops more than they ask for, they turn regular warrants into what they call no-knock warrants."

"So they could have just stormed in without even saying anything." It wasn't a question. I felt into the horror of those hours and imagined them beginning even more violently than they had, without the tiny preamble. In that moment, as crazy as it was, I wished I *had* bought a gun years ago. But I didn't say anything. Instead, I reminded Stefan that we had been talking about who might be out to get us, or one of us. I was afraid of going any deeper into how perverted law enforcement agencies and the judicial system had become. Stefan may have gotten his information from legitimate sources, but if he steeped himself in it enough he would likely become a crank, or chronically depressed, or worse, be targeted for surveillance by the FBI or NSA. And I would be swept along with him, one way or another. Marriage was like that.

And that's when I told him about the threat at the stop sign when I'd been walking Marco, and how the car might have hit us. Stefan was surprisingly calm. It was as if this information was somehow welcome, was a piece of crucial evidence, though what either one of us could do with it, I didn't know.

"I thought the swatting would be it, I didn't really think anything else would happen, like the phone call, and this nut in the car," he said. I must have looked blank, because he explained: "That's what the FBI calls it, 'swatting,' when somebody sics a SWAT team on you and it's fraudulent."

"But swatting's what you do to *flies*."

"Don't blame me for the term," Stefan said.

"Well, I guess that fits. It turns you into an insect."

From another yard, I could hear a lawn mower going, and somewhere else nearby, someone was warming up a grill.

"It definitely wasn't Bullerschmidt in the car," I said, trying to put some pieces together, half-closing my eyes to concentrate. "I would recognize his voice." Which meant that if the dean was involved, he had hired someone to harass us. Was that safe? Wouldn't he be afraid of being exposed? Unless he had some kind of hold over this guy. Or, worse, more than one person was out to make us suffer.

"If it happens again," Stefan said, "you have to get the license plate number."

"And do what? Call the police? The same police somebody turned on us?"

Stefan actually threw up his hands.

"Cheer me up," I asked. "Tell me what Father Ryan said."

"You can call him Ryan."

"I know, I try to. Forget that now. You seemed better when he left, did he give you advice or something? Don't tell me you felt better hearing about East Germany."

"He made me feel safer. He looked me right in the eyes and said very slowly '*They're not coming back.*' It was terrific."

"But how does he know?"

"Because one of his brothers is a cop, up north, and Ryan said that since the warrant didn't pan out, they wouldn't be able to get a second one, no matter how easy it was to get the first. And even if they could, the publicity would be very bad, and we'd have a much better case against them in court."

"Court? I would never sue anybody. It would eat me alive . . . Tell me again what Father—what Ryan said?"

Stefan repeated it, and I echoed the words slowly: "They're not coming back." They made sense. Whatever happened, we wouldn't be facing a night of terror again. That would have to be my mantra. It helped, somewhat. I could already feel the muscles in my neck and shoulders tingling and loosening up. That's when I realized I had been *physically* bracing myself for hours for another crushing raid at our house, another flood of terror and shame.

Stefan grimaced, his mouth twisted, and I thought he was in pain, but then he started to laugh. He stopped as if embarrassed.

"What? What is it?"

"You're the one who always thinks of movies," he said. "Well, I just remembered that scene in *True Lies* when Arnold Schwarzenegger's interrogating his wife—"

"—Jamie Lee Curtis—"

"—in that huge concrete holding pen or whatever, and his voice is all distorted and crazy-sounding."

I was about to ask how that really connected to anything, and then it hit me. I said, "Lucky Bitterman."

He nodded. "Lucky Bitterman."

Bitterman was a fairly recent import to EAR, a graduate of NYU's top-ranked Film Studies program, and Lucky wasn't a nickname; his parents had given him that name because they were inveterate gamblers. Lucky's expertise was thrillers from Hitchcock to Brian de Palma. The department was beefing up its film courses and he'd been hired with tenure on the strength of James Franco as a reference and several screen-play deals. The hiring committee hadn't known how few film deals ever turned into actual films and had been snowed by his apparent promise, his New York hauteur, his Franco connection, and his references to "Marty" Scorsese.

If it sounds hard to believe they could be so gullible and uninformed, a different EAR committee seeking diversity had once hired someone from Indonesia assuming she was Muslim. That was Lucille Mochtar, who had lived across the street from us in a house that was almost a twin of ours. Of course, the committee couldn't ask her religion, but if they had, she would have told them she was a Christian. It hadn't occurred to them anyone in Indonesia *wasn't* a Muslim. Never underestimate the myopia and narcissism of a group of university professors working together.

The film deals had collapsed after Bitterman got to Michiganapolis; James Franco had never accepted an invitation to speak at SUM; and our department and Bitterman were equally disappointed in each other. But thirtyish Bitterman stood out even among our generally sour faculty for the steady bile he poured out on pretty much everyone and everything. He invidiously compared our university to NYU. He called all Michiganders "hicks" and thought the state was a cultural wasteland. He hated both me and Stefan and wasn't afraid to admit it, perhaps because we were also from New York but *liked* living in Michigan. Unless it was that we were a couple. Whatever the reason, he'd called Stefan a hack writer more than once, and told me my Edith Wharton bibliography was a giant Post-It note. I actually thought that was kind of funny, but didn't tell him.

A runner, Bitterman was a lean, handsome, blond, but his mouth was always turned down at the corners, his nose was usually wrinkling in disgust, and seeing him at any time of the year was like being splashed with a pail of scummy pond water.

Why did I think of him? Because Bitterman, who could not have been born with a more fitting name, had recently published a study of Schwarzenegger's thrillers called *Double Trouble*. And even a good review in the *New York Times Book Review* hadn't made him more collegial.

"It might have been him in the car," I said. "I can't be sure it wasn't. I don't know what he drives. I don't think I've ever seen him in the parking lot at Parker Hall."

"That's a good enough place to start," Stefan said.

"The parking lot?"

"No, Bitterman."

"And if it's him?"

"Well, he likes Schwarzenegger so much, remember the line from *Conan the Barbarian* about what is best in life?"

I sure did: "'To crush your enemies, see them driven before you, and hear the lamentation of their women.'"

Stefan gave me a high five, and I thought "Shit, this is dangerous territory." But that didn't stop me from contemplating sweet and lasting revenge.

7

We spent the rest of Thursday watching the *Bourne Trilogy* again, ordered Domino's Brooklyn-style pizza for dinner, and killed two bottles of Chianti. We'd enjoyed the films before, but this time I think both of us connected viscerally to Jason Bourne floating in the sea, getting picked up by that Italian trawler, not knowing who he is or why he remembers the few things he does. That was us after the nighttime raid: confused, isolated, lost.

Stefan watched the three movies in virtual silence, transfixed, but he didn't seem to experience any catharsis by the end of the evening, because the next morning, Friday, he didn't want to get out of bed or even talk about investigating Lucky or anyone.

"*Leave me alone.*" He actually pulled a pillow over his head as if that would make me and the world disappear. I wasn't going to argue with somebody who'd been humiliated so profoundly by the cops, so I walked Marco and then had breakfast by myself. I left Stefan a pot of fresh mocha java coffee and hoped the aroma would finally tempt him downstairs. Marco might manage it, too, because sometimes he'd jump onto the bed and nuzzle your face till you had to admit he was there and that he needed your attention. He was a Westie, and the one time I'd watched the Westminster Dog Show, the announcer said of the breed, "Westies will not be ignored."

I didn't like the idea of Stefan glooming in bed, but I had to get to SUM. I could have walked the ten minutes to campus from our house, but I drove because I felt I needed the safety of metal around me. On the way over, I was startled to realize that we hadn't received any media calls yet. Was it possible the police raid had slipped under the radar? But what about all our neighbors? Wouldn't somebody have notified the *Michiganapolis Tribune* or one of the trashy AM stations? Nowadays everybody wanted to be a mini-celebrity and break a story of some kind, or be interviewed about it.

Campus actually wasn't quite as lush as usual this spring, because of our drought, but even so, it looked appealing, though it wasn't remotely as old as Yale or other eastern schools. It's a vast sprawling place with architecture ranging from sandstone buildings of the 1850s through glass boxes only a few years old, anchored by a core of ugly 1950s buildings of brick construction that was for the most part well landscaped enough to seem inoffensive. I was headed to my office in Parker Hall to consult with my administrative assistant, Celine Robichaux, about fellowship applications. We already had picked someone for this coming year, but we were scheduling people three years out, and there were hundreds of applications.

I say "we" because Celine was my sounding board as much as Stefan when it came to picking the visiting author. As a Wharton scholar, I was drawn to social satirists, and they both helped me widen my range. Her opinion helped a lot because she was astute and widely read but didn't feel any investment in the world of authors and academics, and she was quick to spot phonies, snobs, and potential trouble makers. There was one author of literary novels whose books I enjoyed, but Celine had studied the man's tweets and Facebook posts and this author had bad things to say about almost everyone, especially his students. "We don't need that kind of PR, Nick." Likewise, Celine had suggested we pass on an author of literary thrillers who it turned out would only travel from New York with an entourage including his acupuncturist, his nutritionist, and a tennis pro for whenever he felt the need of a game. And she had also nixed an up-and-coming young author of trashy, amusing "bloodbusters" (vampire-killer novels), because the author, Tiffani Lovegrove, evidently took her last name too literally and had some raunchy photos on Tumblr. They would surely have gotten into the local news and caused a PR tornado if she came to our campus.

I was lucky to have Celine, who was originally from Louisiana, though I didn't detect much of an accent. She was efficient, imaginative, and cheerful in a department of depressives and malcontents, and kind in a university whose values had become increasingly corporate over the years. She helped balance the downsides of teaching at SUM.

Celine was the type of person who seems to be bustling even when she's standing still. I could almost feel the dynamism flowing when our connecting door was open, and definitely experienced that energy whenever she was in my office, radiating from her shoulder-length braids, her glorious smile, and her hugs. Yes, she hugged me—when she was happy or we'd done good work together. I suspected there was muttering about her out there in the sea of cubicles, but they would have to keep it quiet because she was African American and nobody would want to invoke charges of racism.

I parked behind the dilapidated building that until recently had been filled with myriad cracks in the walls and tribes of bats in the halls. Rumors had circulated for years that it would be torn down for a parking structure since parking was always difficult on campus, so the interior restoration was a huge surprise to almost everyone. EAR, like other departments in the College of Arts and Letters, was not a wealthy program that brought in research dollars or alumni donations, so it had been a Cinderella without a prince. Suddenly it hit me: Could the remodeling have been designed to make people forget about the suicide? Would SUM spend that much money to cover up one person's death and the bad PR?

I hadn't been to my office in weeks, and when the elevator doors opened on the cavernous third floor I saw something new hanging over the long front counter. The department had installed a long electronic message board that read "Welcome to EAR. We're here to help you!" That flickered off, then came the date, the temperature outside, and the welcome message again. Insane.

The receptionist was new, and she chirped out, "Hi, how can I be of service?" She was as perky as an old-fashioned weather girl, though she didn't look like one. Her head was shaved, she had a multicolored complicated "sleeve" tattoo on her right arm, and a pierced lower lip. Her clothes were a page out of Madonna's "Like a Virgin" years ago: lace, chains, gloves.

"I teach here. I'm Nick Hoffman."

She glanced down, obviously consulting a list on her tablet. Was this some kind of new security check?

Then she grinned up at me. "Yes you do! I'm Estella!" She shot out an arm to shake my hand as if congratulating me—but if that was for being an EAR faculty member or for meeting her, I didn't know. I did know that Estella was partly there because the renovations had unaccountably not included a wall directory listing where every staffer and faculty member could be found, and it wasn't clear whether we'd end up with one or not. But she was also planted there to make our department seem friendlier. I guess it could have been worse. We could all have been asked to wear t-shirts with smiley faces on them.

I skirted the nearest set of cubicles and headed left to my office at the south end of the floor, keeping my eyes down. Almost everyone who used the cubicles now tended to glare at me, envying my privilege, and I hated that. Though not enough to give up my office or even share it with anyone, of course. But I did feel sorry for all the faculty who had lost old fashioned offices and now had to contend with nothing more than carpeted partitions between them and colleagues they either despised, envied, or both. The fact that the designers had worked in a soothing combination of blue, beige, and gray could not assuage the damage of three dozen faculty members essentially having been evicted, and losing the privilege of privacy and space. I would have hated working in a cubicle under glaring fluorescent lights, hated feeling that everything I did and said was being observed. Even the retrofitting for central air wouldn't have made enough of a difference. Clearly a recipe for menace simmered beneath the surface, and I wouldn't have been surprised if somebody freaked out and had to be carted off for observation.

Celine was in black slacks and a purple cotton Indian-style shirt, and she seemed to have been waiting for me. She rushed forward, grabbed my arm and hustled me into her office which was hung with posters of classic Hitchcock movies like *Vertigo* and *Notorious*. Her hazel eyes were wide with concern and I closed the door behind me, waiting for her to tell me that the assault on my house was in the news and ask if I was okay. I felt my throat tighten.

"Sit down," she said. "Just now, I got a scary phone call from a blocked number. The voice was male, and very strange. He said, '*Nick Hoffman is a dead man*.'"

"Strange how?"

Celine frowned, clearly puzzled that I asked about the voice without reacting to the threat itself. She crossed her arms and hugged herself, trying to remember. "Like the guy in *Scream*, you know, not natural, but . . . well, crazy."

"Did it sound altered, I mean digitally?"

"No, not at all. It was somebody real, and somebody freaky. It did not sound like a joke. This guy was as serious as a heart attack. And hard. You know, like some kind of criminal. Are you in trouble with the Mafia?"

I waved that away. "What did you do?"

"I called campus police, of course, but they said there wasn't anything they could do if the call was blocked. They may send somebody over, but they didn't sound too interested. But *I'm* interested. Nick, is something going on?" Before I could answer, she said, "I've been compiling a list of authors who got nasty when we rejected them. I figured one of them might have been the caller."

I tried not to look relieved. I liked Celine too much to have to lie to her outright, and the idea of another threatening phone call so soon after the first one had unnerved me so much I didn't think I could keep it together if we got anywhere near the truth. I could already feel sweat dripping down between my shoulder blades, making my polo shirt stick to my back. Bullerschmidt had warned us yesterday, and look what had happened already.

"The list is on your desk," she said, and I stood and went through to my office, Celine following. It was an unremarkable space except for that high ceiling, large windows, and the view of lush lawns, sugar maples, and blue sky. For much of the year, you could barely see any buildings because the foliage was so dense, and so I'd had the room painted a soft green when I moved in, and hung posters and framed prints of landscapes by Seurat to capture the soothing feeling of all that verdure.

The disgruntled author list was anything but reflective of calm. I sat down and stared. "This many?" There were two pages of names, along with salient excerpts from their emails or text messages.

Celine demurred. "It's the same people twice, but the second page is organized by threat level." She wasn't kidding. "From low to high."

The Nick Hoffman Fellowship was a hot ticket. The stipend was generous, and the month on campus offered a kind of writer's retreat because the university had let us use the guest wing of the president's Georgian-style house. The work load wasn't tough, but the response from *some* people we'd rejected was. A few of them had told me off, while others had sworn they'd get back at me somehow. Some of the authors in each group shot abuse at me, typically authors who had academic appointments. I'd been called "blind," "provincial," "arrogant," and a host of nastier adjectives by writers who had very high opinions of themselves and obviously thought we had no right to reject their applications. The level of their invective was pretty jejune; I would have expected better insults from writers.

They didn't know it, but in almost every case, the angry response was from someone I had already figured out would not be good to work with, for students or faculty. I didn't just read authors' work. Celine found me interviews, blogs, tweets, anything pertinent they had on Tumblr and Facebook, and public readings from YouTube. It usually wasn't hard to spot the bores, the potential troublemakers, the narcissists, even the drunks. When there was some doubt, we'd also look at their student ratings online if they were teaching.

"Wait a minute," I said. "I don't see Ivan the Terrible on here."

Celine finally smiled.

Ivan Popov was a boozy Bulgarian playwright at one of the smaller state campuses in Michigan who ran a summer creative writing workshop in his native Sofia. He was an irascible, self-important clown, a type that was too typical in academe. Despite the miserable pay at his Bulgarian workshop, and the lousy housing and food, academic writers were dying to get invited since they believed that any European teaching post upped their status. Popov preyed on their vanity, and was notorious for demeaning them when they got there, as well as working them too hard. When it came to our fellowship, he had probably figured being a Michigan author gave him an advantage, so being rejected had enraged him. Popov had actually emailed me, "You'll never see Sofia!" Meaning, I'd never be invited to teach there in his program. As threats go, it was actually funny, since Bulgaria's capital city hadn't ever been on my travel wish list, but he seemed to think it was a death sentence. When I ran into him at a conference afterwards, he'd smirked at me and shook his head as ominously as if he'd managed to alert Bulgarian customs agents to arrest me if I ever dared to fly there on my own.

Celine sat opposite me, her smile fading. "Have you gotten any calls like this at home?" she asked, eyes tight.

I changed the subject: "What am I supposed to do with this list? They're all cranks in one way or another. But *you* were the one who got the phone call. Did you get any sense that one of these people was the caller?"

"I'm not psychic," she said wryly. Celine shook her head and turned her amethyst and diamond engagement ring around and around with three fingers of her right hand. That's what she always did when she was frustrated or annoyed. The list was a kind of blind alley. Phone calls at the office were uncommon. Most communication about faculty matters came via email. Students emailed, too. Which made me think it wasn't an author.

"What are you thinking?" Celine asked, studying my face.

"Why did you mention *Scream*?"

She shrugged. "I guess it's the first thing that popped into my mind. You know, sick phone calls, stalking."

"You think this is a stalker?" Even if I omitted the SWAT team, I couldn't tell her about the incident at the stop sign and the phone call at our house. Or that I suspected Lucky Bitterman—even though she knew about his antagonism toward me and Stefan—because he couldn't have applied for the fellowship. It wouldn't make sense, and she might start asking questions of her own. I had no idea who in town might know about the other night's raid, despite it apparently not having gotten into the news.

And I realized I hadn't thought to note the time of the phone call at home yesterday, so asking her when she'd taken the phone call here in her office wouldn't make a difference. Or would it?

"Isn't this how things would start?" Celine mused. "First a phone call, then some kind of attack, then—"

We both looked up at the same time at the sound of a resonant knock on my thick office door, which opened before either of us said "Come in." It was my old nemesis, Detective Valley, a campus police officer who disliked all faculty members, especially ones like me who got involved in crime and got in his way.

"Professor," he said coldly.

"Detective."

Celine glanced back and forth between us and then rose to leave, but Valley stopped her with a sharp, "No. You I talk to first." He escorted her into her office and closed the door. With the door shut, I could let go, and I closed my eyes, wondering if I was about to get the shakes. The call was shocking enough, but being face-to-face with Valley brought back ugly memories of past confrontations. I had not run into him in six years, and he looked very different. He'd been a tall, lanky, geeky man in suits that looked like they were bought at a consignment shop and had been badly altered, if at all. He was still tall, but he'd gained enough weight or maybe even muscle to look almost threatening—that is, beyond the general intimidation effect that all cops had always seemed to have on me.

Growing up in New York and knowing that the police tended to miss their shots two out of three times had been the kind of fact that made me wary of them, uniformed or not. But it predated knowing those statistics: for some reason, I'd always disliked cops from a very young age, the way some kids are scared of clowns. When I was little, and my mother told me that if I ever got lost and couldn't find her or my father, I should go straight to a policeman, I had burst into tears. It must have been a kind of premonition of the trouble that was waiting for me at SUM. And now, after the night we'd been handcuffed and Stefan dragged off, I never wanted to be in the same room again with any kind of cop.

Celine's door opened and Valley closed it brusquely, so that it slammed, and he came to sit down. Crossing his legs and leaning back as if in a captain's chair, he looked like he meant to stay a long time, whether I wanted him there or not.

"You're a big shot now," he said coldly, eyeing the crammed oak bookcases, the leather desk accessories, and the view as if they all disgusted him. I could have been a French aristocrat facing Robespierre.

I didn't take the bait.

"What are you doing?" he asked. "Why are you attracting crank callers and a SWAT team?" Elbows on the chair arms, he tented his fingers, enjoyed my shock.

8

For a moment, it was like having an out-of-body experience and I could see the two of us sitting in my office, me trapped, him having pounced.

I felt weirdly, calmly distant from the scene, noting the surprisingly sharp cut of his suit, the gray above his ears that was starting to soften the coppery red of his hair. Valley waited for me to say something, trying to intimidate me further by his contemptuous silence. In his mind, professors were miscreants always on the brink of bad behavior, not much better than loutish students who ran wild if SUM teams won a major game and rioted if we lost.

I was dying to turn from the desk and get a Tassimo disc from the credenza behind me and make myself a cup of coffee (without asking if he wanted one, too), anything to not have to look at that smug, angry face. But I wasn't going to let him see how rattled I was that he knew about the cops hitting our house, and turning away would surely prove I needed a time out.

"You look good," I said.

He squinted so hard his eyes must have hurt. "What?"

"You're working out, aren't you? You must be. Your delts are definitely bigger. That suit does not look like the shoulders are padded."

Now *he* was the one off-balance, since I had never complimented him before, and with some men, saying anything to them about their bodies feels invasive and threatening, whether you were gay or not. I had correctly guessed he was one of them, because he looked away, distressed or discomfited. That made me even more determined not to give any ground. I wasn't the same person he had interrogated years ago. I was a full professor and my name was attached to a prestigious fellowship. I wouldn't call myself a big shot, but I wasn't a nobody, either. This wasn't about speaking truth to power, it was about not being intimidated.

To my delight, Valley finally caved. "What do you know about this phone call?"

"Just what my assistant told me."

He nodded skeptically, his narrow chin like a weapon. "Have you been getting other calls here?"

"None." That was true, but only part of the truth, of course. And if he asked about other calls anywhere else, I would have to lie.

"Why would someone be threatening you?"

I explained the possibility of a rejected writer: "Authors live with constant disappointment, and it doesn't take much to push one over the edge. Even a bad review could do it, so not getting the chance to earn $25,000 you feel you deserve and maybe even fantasized about spending, that could be a pretty strong catalyst."

"You're all crazy," he said, upper lip curling in contempt. "So what about your . . . partner? Could he do something like that?"

I snapped at Valley: "You're saying Stefan called the office to threaten *me*? Are you trying to turn this into a domestic dispute? That's bullshit."

He shrugged those newly sturdy shoulders of his and uncrossed his legs, folding his long hands in his lap. "You'll have to report what happened to the phone company. And your assistant needs to fill out a police report at our headquarters. But I have to warn you, people like whoever called, they're not morons even if they are wacko. They plan ahead. They watch the crime shows. They know what to do. So even tracing the call might not tell us anything. There are lots of ways to hide who they are."

"Basically, you're telling me it's a waste of time." I knew that already, but I didn't want him to realize I'd already worked it out myself. I hope I sounded frustrated enough. It was very quiet in the office; the whole campus was quiet with most of the students gone. I could hear the ticking of the antique brass carriage clock Stefan had given me for one birthday, and the air whooshing through the air conditioning vents. I was waiting for Valley to come back to the SWAT team. I didn't want to raise it myself. Not to him, not to anyone, and yet I was eager to find out how he knew.

That wasn't going to happen. Not right then, anyway. He slapped his knees as if he was in a Western and rose. "You know what you need to do," he said somewhat obscurely, and he left via Celine's office. What did he mean? Despite trying to stay calm, I felt unnerved by his visit, and I wished I had some Valium in the office.

Celine bustled in, mimicking the stinkeye Valley always gave me. I laughed at her imitation of his glare, partly out of exhaustion. I didn't care much about hiding the truth from Valley, but I liked and respected Celine. And I felt sorry that she had been harassed, even indirectly.

She cocked her head at me. "What's with the stiff?"

"We have a history."

"I gathered."

"And he's not, shall we say, open to diversity."

"He's a bigot." She shrugged. "Okay, then. Let's get to work," she said, as if offering me a vacation from trouble. We spent over an hour discussing some YouTube readings we'd both watched and were in agreement that the three writers I'd been considering this week were all duds. Their books were great, they were all personable enough, but they didn't engage with their audiences and their Q&A sessions were dreadful. All three seemed profoundly uncomfortable even though they were well-known. Maybe because of that?

"Introverts," Celine ventured. "I like being married to one. But I wouldn't want to take a workshop with an 'inny' or sit there and try to listen to one—I'd go to sleep!"

"Can you get started on the letters?" I handed her my notes. Though I'd developed a form rejection letter, each one was always personalized with references to the author's work I'd liked. And if I hadn't liked any of their books, I made sure to mention an interview, a film adaptation, whatever I could come up with. It might not be much to soften the blow, but it was better than nothing. I'd lived with an author for over twenty years and I knew that rejection letters were likely to feel poisonous, so I tried to make mine as anodyne and even cheerful as possible. I know it was like going vegan to slow global warming, but at least it was something.

On the short drive home, I had the distinct feeling that the same black car from the stop sign was following me. I thought it was one of those new Cadillac XTSs with the distinctive grill, a car I'd seen a lot around town because it was made in Michiganapolis and very popular that summer. This one seemed to be following behind me for more than a few blocks, making every turn I did, but keeping far enough back so I couldn't make out the driver's face. When traffic (such as it was) cleared, and I slowed down to make a right turn, whoever it was sped up to make a left and screeched off too fast for me to be sure what had been going on or even if it was a Caddy. Michiganapolis was filled with bad drivers, so maybe it meant nothing at all, but with two ominous phone calls in a row and the threat at the stop sign, I was primed for the worst. Yet I couldn't have told anyone for sure what make the car had been; I was too rattled and edgy to be a calm, reliable witness.

Stefan was out of bed and dressed when I got home. Good signs. He had started making dinner. Even better. But he hadn't gotten very far. I could tell he had planned on Eggplant Rollatini, one of our summer favorites, since I saw eggplants, fresh basil, and the makings of tomato sauce on one counter. Stefan himself was sitting cross-legged on the floor, Marco in his lap. Marco wagged his tail hello, but didn't move. Eyes dead, Stefan looked shell-shocked and was clearly the one who needed canine attention.

I apologized for being late and not having called. Then I asked, "How was Mass?"

Stefan looked away. "I didn't go."

Now that was a very bad sign, since Father Ryan was celebrating it that day. Stefan had become a regular at the weekday Masses, in addition to going Sunday mornings. He almost always returned calmer, usually talking about the homily. Sometimes he shared the intense feelings of gratefulness and connection he felt there, but not often. He didn't have to. I'd read his memoir *New Home* and understood how for the first time in his life, he felt spiritually grounded, though I myself couldn't identify with Jesus or anything connected to the Catholic Church. It hadn't been something we spoke much about until he wrote the book, but we did when I read the early drafts, and I'd admired his courage. He was the son of Holocaust survivors, and yet he'd broken with his past, their past. And because he was well-known as a Jewish author, he had risked alienating his audience. Who knew he'd gain a much larger one with the memoir? Readers loved the cool, brainy prose that many reviewers compared to Joan Didion's. I suspect they were surprised by his tone, given the controversial subject of his book—at least for some people. After all, according to some studies, fully a quarter of all Americans changed from their religion of birth to something else.

Before I could say anything now to lift Stefan out of his stupor, the doorbell rang and his eyes widened.

"It's okay," I said. "Remember Father Ryan? Repeat after me: *They're not coming back.*"

He repeated it in a low voice, like someone heavily sedated.

I left him there. Waiting at the front door was one of our elderly neighbors, Binnie Berrigan, holding a domed Tupperware cake plate. Binnie went to Stefan's church, was in her eighties, widowed, a raging progressive, and a devotee of hiking and biking vacations. She was short, lean, with a white braid down her back, and given to flowing Indian print skirts with matching tops and chunky turquoise necklaces. She'd been arrested many times over the years and was proud of her protests against Vietnam, the Cambodia bombing, nuclear power, the wars in Iran and Afghanistan. "As long as they keep electing idiots, somebody's got to hold them to account," she liked to say. "I knew Nixon was a chiseler from day one, and little Bush was a bum."

It was a sign of how troubled Stefan was that Marco hadn't trotted to the door, since he loved Mrs. Berrigan. Marco knew Stefan needed taking care of.

"Nick, dear, I won't come in, but when I didn't see Stefan at Mass today, I made you boys your favorite sour cream coffee cake." She handed over the plate. Despite myself, I looked behind her, wondering who might be watching our front door. "You're good boys, both of you, I know that. If police come to your house the way they did the other night, I know it's a mistake or a lie."

I breathed in deeply, trying not to tear up, and she patted my arm.

"Did they hurt you?" she asked.

I shook my head, and tried to say something, but she guessed it. "Yes, I know, it's on the inside. I won't tell you it's going to pass, because nobody can know that. The first time I got dragged off a picket line I thought I was a hero, but after being roughed up and held in jail for forty-eight hours, I felt like a worm. Just take care of each other, okay?" She turned and strode down the steps and off along the street to her Cape Cod, the only one on our street. As I closed the door, I had the eerie feeling I was being watched, and I heard a car speed down our street, where the limit was twenty-five miles per hour. When I opened the door again, the car was gone. *Paranoid*, I thought. *You will always be paranoid now, till the day you die.* My beautiful, peaceful home had become a cul-de-sac of dread. But I had to suppress what I was feeling—right then, anyway, to deal with Stefan.

I brought the cake into the kitchen and relayed Binnie's message. Stefan moaned, "Everyone at church will know! I can't ever go back."

I set down the cake on the table littered with opened sections of the *New York Times*, and crouched by his side. "Listen, they *love* you at St. Jude's, I've seen it at the Christmas parties we've gone to, they all think you're special. And even if they didn't, church is the best place for you to go! You feel at home there. You wrote a book about it, remember?"

He smiled faintly, and Marco headed off his lap for a drink of water. "Is that Binnie's coffee cake?" Stefan asked, sounding marginally more positive, and as if I hadn't already told him. I nodded, and he rose to take off the dome. I brought out plates, forks, and a cake knife and we sat at the island to have dessert before dinner, which seemed a harmless reversal of order after what we'd been through the past few days. I needed to get my footing back, somehow. I wished I had some kind of large, detail-ridden project that could still my murky free-floating sense of panic and help me focus on something constructive. But all I had right then was a crumbly, sweet, coffee cake made with freshly ground cinnamon. It could have been worse.

Well, probably not, because I had to tell him about the call Celine had gotten, and that I'd had a brief interview with Detective Valley. He took that like a punch-drunk fighter. He sat there, playing with his fork, shoulders hunched, eyes drawn inward, so I fed Marco his dinner, let him out into the yard, and decided to make the eggplant dish myself. I cheated and used prepared sauce for the bottom of the baking dish, but went ahead and sliced and blanched the eggplants, pureed some cottage cheese, mixed in the Parmesan, mozzarella, garlic, lemon zest, nutmeg, pepper and salt. I talked to him about the rest of my time at the office, discussed the three authors, one of whom he'd been on a panel with.

I was surprised when he ignored the gossip and said, "Valley's back? I hate that man. He should be shot." He pronounced his sentence dully, as if talking about cleaning up a messy garage, not offing another human being. But strangely, that made me think of the gun shop I'd visited years ago, the feel of a pistol in my hand, the sense of threatening power and strength I hadn't expected. What would I do if I had one?

Clearing the table of the *Times*, I noticed one section was open to a book review of something called *Erroneous*, and the author's photo shocked me. It was Stone Castro-Hirsch, a mercurial, acerbic, foul-mouthed essayist who edited a Jewish literary magazine called *Nu?* (Yiddish for "So what?") He had once asked Stefan for an essay at a point in his career when Stefan had stopped writing "on spec"—that is, without a definite commitment to publish. Stefan was always happy to work with editors to get pieces where they needed to be, but Stone not only rejected the piece outright, he slammed Stefan in an email: "This is the worst shit I've ever read by any author living or dead. I can't believe you thought I'd waste my time with something this hopeless." I'd read the essay and it wasn't Stefan's best work, but Stone's comments struck me as unhinged.

Stefan had fumed for a few days, composing and recomposing a blistering email reply which he wisely never sent. I urged him not to, since I assumed Stone was volatile and troubled, and definitely worth staying away from. He was the kind of person who couldn't fart without mentioning it on Facebook and was notorious there for defriending people for the most trivial reasons, or none at all.

But despite Stefan's silence (or because of it?), somehow Stone took a dislike to him and every now and then we'd hear he had trashed Stefan somewhere in print or even at a party of litwits. I skimmed the *Times* review now: the book was a collection of Stone's own essays from *Nu?* with one written just for the book, called "Traitors." It apparently singled out Stefan. There was a quote in the review about Stefan's conversion to Catholicism as "shameful, cowardly, revolting, superstitious, and ignorant," and Stefan himself was branded "one of the worst enemies the Jewish people have ever faced in their history, finishing what Hitler started."

Stefan and his publisher had gotten a fair amount of hate mail a few years back when his conversion memoir came out, but the overwhelming response by reviewers and readers had been laudatory. Invitations to speak had descended from across the country and he had to hire a graduate student to help him keep track of all the requests and sort the ones he found most interesting. Most Jewish newspapers and magazines—including *Nu?*—had quietly ignored the book, not wanting to give him any more publicity than he was getting already, since it sold close to half a million copies in hard cover, and even more as an ebook.

Stefan came over to the table. "I heard last year that Stone told an audience I was the author he most detested. He said I was despicable and didn't deserve to live."

I was surprised he could be so casual about what sounded dangerously close to a death threat. "You never mentioned him saying that."

Stefan looked exhausted. "Nick, it's not important, he's a crank, he's a malcontent. He sees all these people around him in New York who are richer, more famous, better looking, who get better press, and he can't stand it. But he doesn't want to pick a fight with somebody there, so he takes shots at people like me outside his circle."

The oven timer rang for the Rollatini and when I turned from the table, I said, "What if this essay was just *part* of his plan? What if he's out to really hurt you, for whatever sick reason? What if he's the one following me—" I stopped, mortified that I'd added to Stefan's burden. He cocked his head at me and I told him about the car I thought was behind me earlier. But I didn't give him a chance to react. "Stone is clearly obsessed with you, Stefan. If he's the one stalking us, you've got to do something, call the police."

As soon as I said those last words, I regretted my stupidity.

He grimaced sourly. "You're kidding, right? You think I'd call the police for *anything*?"

"No, sorry. That was a reflex. I'm really sorry."

Later that night, with Stefan snoozing in the living room in front of an *NCIS* episode on TV that we'd seen half a dozen times, I couldn't help myself. I googled Stone, well aware that if he knew what I was doing, Stefan might hit me with one of his favorite Gospel quotations, "Who can touch pitch, and not be defiled by it?"

And after wading through five minutes of muck, I discovered that Stone was a lot closer than New York, ominously close. He was teaching in a summer writing workshop at SUM's small branch campus in Ludington, just a few hours northwest of Michiganapolis.

We had a condo in Ludington.

I couldn't believe this was a coincidence.

9

I loved Ludington, and thinking of that creep in one of my favorite Michigan locales really troubled me.

Situated on Lake Michigan, Ludington was a scenic little town, with a touch of New England charm to it—in my eyes, anyway. It had once been the hub of the Michigan lumber industry and a major port on the Great Lakes. Nowadays its business was tourism, boating, fishing, camping, and hunting. With fewer than ten thousand citizens, it was celebrated for its pretty beaches and harbor, and its historic lighthouse was ranked Michigan's most beautiful. After more than a century, Ludington still had a working car ferry line—the S.S. *Badger*—that took you across to Wisconsin.

We'd visited Ludington now and then since moving to Michigan, and before the stock market crashed in 2008, Stefan and I had bought a condo there after selling the cabin we owned a few hours further north near the larger town of Charlevoix. The upkeep on the cabin had become too burdensome: the electricity went out too often, pipes froze, the roof was going, the foundation cracking. Once his father and stepmother— who had given him the cabin—were dead, Stefan didn't want to go up there anymore. I understood and didn't mind having a shorter drive for weekend getaways. Selling it was easy even though it needed work, because it had some prime frontage on the lake.

Ludington wasn't as wealthy a town as Charlevoix, didn't have a plethora of great restaurants, but it still had Lake Michigan and the gorgeous sunsets. We could watch those from our loft bedroom. There was only one large room downstairs with an open sleek kitchen, and the full bathroom on that floor wasn't very big, but all of that was fine with us since we hadn't bought it to entertain guests. It was a true getaway.

In Ludington, we slept late, walked the beach, biked, and generally acted as if we were from much further away than Michiganapolis.

We'd bought it before getting Marco, and the condo didn't allow pets, but he was very happy at the kennel where he was boarded and a favorite with the staff because of his sweet disposition. We never stayed for more than a long weekend, which was usually enough time to help us chill out, and we'd been coming there long enough to have our favorite bistro, Blue Moon, which served the Canadian specialty poutine, and our favorite funky coffee shop, Redolencia.

But how was there a writing workshop at the Ludington campus of SUM that I hadn't heard about? I was on sabbatical, but wasn't *that* much out of touch, was I? And why hadn't Stefan been involved as SUM's writer-in-residence? Then I realized that Stefan must have been aware, which was why he had offered so many vague excuses a week ago when I suggested we take some time at the condo. He didn't want to be in town when it was happening.

I took Marco out one last time and then headed up to bed, figuring Stefan would wake up in the living room eventually and follow.

Yes, I knew about the workshop," Stefan admitted sleepily at breakfast Saturday morning, only marginally more present than the day before. "And I didn't say anything, because Stone makes you crazy."

Stefan wasn't exaggerating. Once he'd calmed down about Stone trashing his essay all those years ago, I'd grabbed the torch of resentment and kept it burning. I was furious enough that if I had seen one of Stone's books in a local bookstore, I would have slipped it behind others so nobody would find it. As my cousin Sharon liked to say: "You're a Taurus. You guys can simmer for years." Stone was my personal allergen. I'd hear or read his name and I'd feel miserable and pissed off. His name worked on me like the stench off the clothes of a chain smoker.

"I was invited by the arts group in Ludington that's renting space from SUM at that little conference center," Stefan said after pouring himself more coffee. "And I asked who else was coming to do workshops and readings. When I heard Stone had already accepted, I passed. And then I didn't want to think about it or talk about it."

Spoken like a true introvert. Extroverts like me have to *work* at keeping things to ourselves.

"So all this shit starts happening to us," I said. "And your nemesis turns out to be in Michigan, and nearby? Tell me that's not suspicious." I'd been at the same place before—*we* had, actually—mentally slipping a seemingly ordinary person into the frame of a mug shot.

Stefan forked up some of his asparagus omelet, chewed thoughtfully, and said, "How would he associate Ludington with us?"

"Because you've written about it, remember? For that anthology about Michigan small towns? The one that won a prize and was reviewed in the *Times*?"

"Oh, right. I forgot." Stefan's popularity had exploded after his memoir came out and he was constantly getting asked to contribute to anthologies, to do blurbs for new books, to contribute to publishing-related projects or causes.

"Somebody like that," I said, "hoovers down the *Times* and the *New York Review of Books* and the *New Yorker*. You know the type. And he hates you. He probably memorizes your good reviews and figures out ways to undermine them."

"You think he's that vicious."

"I know he is. He sent you the craziest, nastiest rejection you ever got in your whole career."

"Granted. But how would he turn us into the target of a SWAT team?"

"How would anyone do it? It happens. You told me. Vanessa told us. Tips come in all the time. The cops end up targeting the wrong people by mistake. Sometimes it's faulty intelligence, and sometimes they're set up to do it. That's what happened. We need to go to Ludington."

Stefan shook his head.

I was not backing down. "Listen, if Stone is behind everything that's been going on, I want to confront him. I want to look him in the eye."

"And do what? Get him to confess like in a mystery novel? The villain only does that when he's about to kill somebody and he's gloating."

"Stone is *always* gloating. He's a smug sonofabitch. He's a nasty piece of work and he's made a career out of it, trashing people he isn't going to need for favors." That was the draw of his nasty little magazine, of course. People read it for *schadenfreude*, enjoying eviscerations in reviews and articles of writers they envied. It was a niche market, and surprisingly successful.

"I wouldn't mind getting away," Stefan said, eyes distant. "But what about Marco? You know the kennel is usually pretty booked in the warm weather, especially on weekends."

I'd thought of that already. Binnie Berrigan had a miniature poodle who got along beautifully with Marco when we met on walks. Binnie had more than once offered to take care of Marco if we ever needed her to. I reminded Stefan of that and said, "Let me call her and see if she's available the next couple of days." I did, and she was.

Binnie was our nicest neighbor, aside from Vanessa, whom we barely knew, though she had shared unbelievable intimacy with us because of our night of terror and its aftermath. The rest of our nearest neighbors weren't dog people, so we didn't interact much. "Fred and Ethel" were our neighbors to the south, an elderly retired couple who were always squabbling in the garden, each one digging up and moving flowers and shrubs as if shifting furniture around a room, and always without consulting the other one. Their name was actually Kurtz, and that and their quarrelsomeness reminded us of the Mertzes on *I Love Lucy*.

We never spoke since I'd had a run-in with Mr. Kurtz a few years back when I was walking Marco and he peed on the Kurtz's green plastic trash can down by the curb. Mr. Kurtz came shouting across his lawn, "You always let your dog do that! I have to carry that bin! I have to touch it!" I didn't point out that Marco was too short to pee all the way up on the handles. I apologized and said it wouldn't happen again, but he kept yelling at me even as I made my way down the block. "People like you spoil this neighborhood!" And a few minutes later he drove by me super-fast in his Dodge Caravan as if to scare me, or at least show me how angry he was.

An equally charmless couple lived on our other side, Maude and Lewis Priebus, professors of music at SUM who only associated with their colleagues. After living there ten years, they had never had us over for coffee or a drink, even though we'd invited them to more than one of our parties—and they'd come. Both always wore black. She played viola and he was a pianist, so the music we heard from their windows was enjoyable, at any rate, especially when they had colleagues over for chamber music rehearsals. Across the street were mostly new people, including Vanessa, who had the house our friends and colleagues Lucille and Didier had owned before taking jobs in Canada. We missed them, and other people we'd gotten to know too briefly before they moved away. Living in a college town was great for the lack of traffic, the slower pace of life and everything that went with that, but it also meant your friends often moved on to better jobs someplace bigger and more exciting. I wondered how long an East Coaster like Vanessa would last in Michiganapolis.

Stefan had been cleaning up while I spoke to Binnie and when I got back to the kitchen, he said, "We'll talk about Stone and Lucky and anyone else we can think of on the ride to the condo, okay?" He went off to pack a bag.

I was glad to be in my SUV, a terrifically comfortable trip car, driving away from the home that no longer seemed safe. I imagined people who'd suffered through fires, hurricanes, or tornadoes felt the same way. The false sense of invulnerability that makes you watch other people's disasters on TV with the knowledge this could never happen to you—well, that was gone, sanded clean away. And so Stefan and I were on the road, however briefly, perhaps doing what Tom does in *The Glass Menagerie*, "attempting to find in motion what was lost in space."

For a while, we were silent, just enjoying the distance that grew between us and home, the relative peace and quiet of the highway. We didn't talk, as I thought we would. Then Stefan put in half a dozen CDs and we blasted classic rock: Led Zeppelin, The Stones, Cream, David Bowie, The Allman Brothers. I don't know about him, but I felt young and reckless, I felt free. We actually sang along to some songs, making lousy, fun harmony.

And when we drove into Ludington on Route 10 heading west to Lake Michigan, I felt becalmed. Something about driving through the cordon of mini-malls, lumber shops, motels, fast food outposts and then hitting the main street of Robber Baron mansions that had all been turned into guest houses was inevitably soothing for me. All that colorfully painted gingerbread was such a sharp contrast to what we had just passed through, as were the one- and two-story commercial buildings with ornate decorative Victorian stone work around the windows or along the roof lines, even displaying the dates of construction carved in relief by proud architects.

We passed our favorite building: the big square sandstone courthouse from 1893 whose Romanesque revival style and tower could make you think of castles and sieges and torture chambers if you were in the wrong mood. In the right mood, it was dramatic and romantic, and we still treasured the night a few years back when we'd walked by and the moon was hanging so low in the sky that it seemed like a reflection of the huge white clock face up in the tower.

At the end of Ludington's main drag we turned right onto North Lakeshore Drive and were quickly pulling up to our condo, which was a short walk from the harbor formed by Pere Marquette Lake. The condo was in a building that had formerly been a brewery back in the early 1900s: a solid red brick building decorated with square towers at each corner. The thick old walls made for sublime quiet when it was converted into condos a decade ago. Our bi-level condo was only 750 square feet but the fourteen-foot ceilings and the view made it impossible to feel cramped. Reached by an open stepped stairway, the tower bedroom with windows on three sides was what had sold me almost instantly. Stefan and I had once stayed at a hotel in the Loire Valley that was a nineteenth-century version of a Renaissance chateau, and our bedroom there had been in a turret. So this place reminded me immediately of one of the most romantic vacations we ever had, and I was thrilled to have a piece of the past imported so easily into our present. Stefan said it reminded him of the books he had read about King Arthur as a child, so for him, too, the building evoked something deep.

The décor was very spare and urban, all redone after Stefan's memoir started hitting best-seller lists. Stefan had shopped at Herman Miller in Grand Rapids and bought us two black leather Eames chairs and an Eames sofa, which were arranged around a large black and white marble square that served as a coffee table. Near the kitchen we had a round white Eames table and four matching molded chairs. The floors were red oak, and the walls everywhere were bare; the ones that weren't exposed brick we'd had painted apricot. The colors glowed thanks to light streaking in from all the rounded-top windows and Deco-style hanging globe lights. My cousin Sharon had only seen photos and said it was a bit severe for her taste, but I think she might have felt differently if she'd seen the warmth of the light and the unobstructed views from our bedroom, which was in effect a tiny penthouse. Stefan and I found the simplicity restful, and there were no pictures or knickknacks to dust or clean.

We always kept the Liebherr freezer and fridge well-stocked, so we defrosted some ground lamb for lunch, making burgers with blue cheese. Neither one of us had grown up in a kosher home, but even now, people would sometimes see me mix meat and dairy or have bacon at a restaurant brunch and wonder about it. For some reason, non-Jews seem fixated on the laws of keeping kosher, or maybe that's about the only aspect of Jewish culture they're cognizant of, aside from the fact that we don't celebrate Christmas (of course, I did now, with Stefan). We each drank a Warsteiner with our burger, and while I felt invigorated, the beer seemed to knock Stefan out. He went upstairs for a nap, and I told him I was going out to explore, but I had another agenda. He was too sleepy and worn out by the week's stress to suspect anything.

The tiny branch campus of SUM was actually one square, four-story building set in the middle of its own tree-lined parking lot overlooking Pere Marquette Lake, which Ludington clustered along and which also connected to Lake Michigan. The building had a gorgeous setting; too bad it looked as bland inside and out as a pile of photocopying paper. SUM had bought the structure from a Bible college that had gone bankrupt (after an embezzlement scandal involving its president and founder). So it was ready-made for an extension campus since it already had offices, classrooms, even a cafeteria. Stefan and I had both been invited to teach summer classes there before, but we'd declined because we didn't want Ludington to be anything more than an escape for us. Associating it with teaching, no matter how good the students were or how much fun we had, would have been a bit of a buzzkill.

I drove there cautiously because, being Saturday, the sidewalks were jammed, the streets were choked with cars, and dozens of vacationers crossed at every light. But I didn't mind. Even when Ludington was crowded, it still felt open to me compared to Michiganapolis, which wasn't huge, but the state capital nonetheless. Ludington was hardly Big Sky country, but the low elevation of the buildings, the views of Lake Michigan, the good weather, all typically made me feel I had escaped.

I suppose I could have walked from our condo, but I was concerned about making a quick getaway if I needed to, not that my thinking had advanced any further than that. I had abandoned my half-formed idea of confronting Stone and figured I would just do some snooping to begin with, perhaps even spy on him from a distance, maybe even follow him. After all, hadn't he been following me?

But the urgency of my quest had diminished the closer I got. I confess that I felt a little more relaxed, and it was more than being away from home, or the beer. The weather was perfect: sunny and mid-70s with a slight breeze, and the bright skies were filled with wheeling and diving gulls. I know people from out of state can grouse that Lake Michigan isn't the Atlantic or even the Gulf of Mexico, but it looks big enough to me since I can't see the other shore. And the lake can get rough enough to make enormous waves.

When I pulled into the campus parking lot, which formed a U around the squat little building with its weirdly Gothic-letter SUM sign over the main doors which were glass, there were dozens of cars there. I parked and prowled among them, and then saw, off by itself, a black Cadillac XTS. I approached it carefully across the blacktop, as if it might start up by itself and chase me like in a Stephen King nightmare. My heart was beating a little faster now as I re-experienced the feeling of thinking I was being followed the other day. The XTS was a low-slung luxury sedan, with all kinds of sophisticated sensors for safety I'd read about in various magazines, and I vaguely remembered something un-usual about its lights. I wondered if it was even filming me as I crept around the car, looking in through the clear front windows to see—see what? If Stone had a photo of our house in Michiganapolis? A map with a big red circle marking our street? What evidence would anyone leave lying around on the front seat of his car?

But then wasn't he arrogant enough to take that kind of risk? And didn't criminals always think they were smarter than anyone else? He sure thought he was smarter than Stefan, and more talented as a writer.

"Hey, asshole, get away from my car!" someone shouted from behind me.

When I jumped back from the passenger-side window and turned, it was Stone, his narrow face red and twisted with rage.

Standing twenty feet away, he growled, "Wait! I know who you are! What the *fuck* are you doing here? Are you stalking me?"

10

Since the day he'd torn into Stefan's essay and sent the abusive email, I'd developed a mental image of Stone angrily typing away in some dank New York basement apartment like an unsavory conspiracy theory blogger afraid that his coffee pot was bugged. Sure, I'd seen some publicity photos of him, but I imagined him grungier, unshaven and smelly, like he slept in his clothes and rarely showered. That was clearly a fantasy. Six feet tall like me, but rock star slim, Stone looked annoyingly hip in a tight white shirt with the short sleeves stretched by his ropy biceps, loosened skinny black tie, black jeans and black crocodile slip-ons with no socks.

Just moments before, the world had seemed large and open; now it was very small and cramped, a tunnel with me at one end and Stone at the other. As he approached, he whipped out his key fob and pressed it. LED lights unexpectedly came on all around the car—including the door handles and rearview mirrors—in some complex sequence that was like a bomb being armed in a sci-fi movie. I was startled and distracted by the light show—which was what he intended, I'm sure—and turned partly away from Stone. That was a mistake.

He rushed me and grabbed at my left shoulder. I whirled around, clamped my hands on his arms, pinning them to his sides, and shoved him hard against the side of his Cadillac, which did not start yowling. It may have sophisticated security lighting, but it did not seem primed to deal with a vengeful college professor. Not that I cared if an alarm went off *outside* my head; inside I felt all the clangor of fire trucks and ambulances rushing to a blaze. More noise wouldn't have bothered me.

My face was hot, my senses so alive it was hallucinatory. I could smell his fear as intensely as I could smell his Cool Water cologne. I could *see* it. It sounds crazy, but I could have sworn I even *felt* the blood rushing through the veins in his arms.

Even though I was easily thirty pounds heavier and more muscular than ever before from swimming laps five days a week, he struggled and tried to knee me in the groin. I blocked his leg and stomped on one of his expensive shoes, grinding my sneakered heel into it.

"You're fucking crazy!" he yelled. "I'm going to get a restraining order on you. I'm going to sue your ass and *crush* you."

Stone was practically foaming at the mouth and I could smell the coffee he'd been drinking, even the artificial sweetener he'd used. I wanted to hurt him more badly than I already had, head butt him or punch him in the stomach till he passed out or puked or both. I had never felt such an onrush of violence in me before—and I loved it.

Each time he tried to struggle, I grabbed him tighter, feeling like a vigilante cornering a thief. I understood in those moments the thrill of being a bully, of dominating and humiliating somebody weaker than yourself—and I wasn't remotely ashamed of what I was doing. It was new, it was amazing, it was revenge for having been so powerless.

Despite his rage, or maybe because of it, I could tell he was surprised that I'd manhandled him. His deep blue eyes were scared, and they were very guilty eyes; there was no other way to read them. I was dead sure of that.

We were alone in the sunny parking lot, and tightening my grip even further on his muscled forearms, I said, "You're a liar and a thug. You've been following me, harassing me and Stefan. Admit it! And you set us up for the SWAT team invading our house. I know you did." What would it take to get him to confess?

"I don't know what the fuck you're talking about. You're delusional!"

"You're driving a black XTS. I've been followed by a black XTS." At least I thought so.

"And there's only one of these in the whole fucking state? Are you on crack or something? Why the fuck would I follow you?"

"Because you hate Stefan."

"I hate all lousy writers!"

"No, you're jealous of him."

"Are you fucking kidding me? Publishing is full of losers like Stefan. Give me a break."

"Stefan's a loser? His memoir was a best seller."

"Right. Christian nut jobs bought his book," he sneered. "That's a great audience. He's a fucking joke. He was a nobody before his memoir, and now he's a clown. His book is crap, it's wishful thinking, sentimental noxious crap."

If our confrontation had swept me up like a roof in a tornado, I was suddenly dropped to earth. I let Stone go, stepping well back. I'm not sure why. He shook himself like a dog emerging from a bath.

I suddenly felt disgusted with myself, as if the contempt on his face had been painted there by me, as if he were some dark aspect of myself I was getting too good a look at. I wondered what the hell I was doing there not just roughing somebody up, but arguing now about a book. A *book*! That was truly bizarre.

Stone rubbed his arms, shaking his head at me. "You're a pathetic wannabe," he said. "All you academics are the same. You think teaching can fill you up. Nothing can. You live with a writer because you're a parasite. Too bad the writer you live with is emptier than you are." He picked up the key fob he had dropped when I grabbed him and limped quickly around to the driver's side, opened the door and slipped in, driving off before I could say anything or even *think* of what to say. I watched him disappear, wondering if he was going to find the police station and report me. Should I stay there? Would leaving be seen as "flight" and make me guiltier than I already was?

I couldn't believe it. Just a few days ago Stefan had been taken away to jail for something he hadn't done, and now I might be *really* jailed because I *was* a criminal. I was guilty of assault, and who knew what other legal charges the cops could throw at me.

I trailed back to my own car, sweating and mortified. I got in slowly, awkwardly, started it, but didn't go anywhere, turned up the air conditioning and pointed every possible vent at my face to cool off. I'd never lost control like that before in my life, never. I had never hurt someone deliberately and enjoyed it, *reveled* in it. Had I already become what I hated? Had being victimized by cops turned me into a monster so quickly? What I had just done was reprehensible. There was no sugarcoating it, no excuse. It was assault. If he did sue me and take me to court, how would I defend myself? I couldn't prove any of my charges, and even if I could, that didn't give me the right to attack him.

The SWAT team had made me completely slip my moorings. Stefan would be furious, and rightly so. And I couldn't imagine what my parents would say if this incident came out, or Sharon, or anyone who liked and respected me.

But in the midst of my recriminations, something else bubbled up: Why had I backed off? Was it what Stone had said about Stefan's literary standing that had made the difference? Was that a claim I couldn't contest, something I half-believed myself? I had told Stefan I loved his memoir when I read the early drafts, but that was when his conversion was so new that I felt off-balance, hesitant, and even threatened. I don't know if I could have read it with a clear mind and honest intentions. I didn't want to say anything negative that might push him away since I was worried enough that his becoming a Catholic would separate us.

Whatever the subject, if you live with a writer, can you ever truly judge their work? Be objective? You've seen the struggle behind the book, the career anxieties and disappointments, the external pressure to produce, the more insidious internal pressure to make people notice this new book if the previous one has somehow been slighted. Puzzling over all this, I started to feel worse than I had been feeling already.

I'd been exposed. Stone was insidious, and his charge about Stefan's book wasn't haphazard. He had intuited my doubts and gotten under my skin as readily as if I'd confessed them to him, drunk at a bar one night, and forgotten all about it the next morning. Only a sociopath had that uncanny ability to manipulate people's weaknesses. And here I thought roughing him up had given me the advantage, had made me a winner, however briefly. He'd probably expected me to get overly physical as soon as he'd discovered me near his car, and had played me as easily as he'd switched on all those pretty lights on his XTS. What a moron I was.

And then something even more terrible hit me: What if I'd backed off because I was starting to have doubts about Stone being the culprit?

I probably sat there a good fifteen minutes before I was calm enough to drive to the condo. I had to tell Stefan what I'd done, and I dreaded his reaction, fearing a look of contempt as corrosive as Stone's.

I was about to call you," he said, when I let myself in. He was sprawled on the couch, looking more contented than he'd been since before our lives were pulled inside out by the police.

I didn't delay by making coffee or fixing us drinks or asking if he wanted to go out for a tapas dinner. I sat down at the other end of the couch and told him what had just happened with as much detail as if I'd been giving a deposition. When I was done, Stefan was grinning at me so broadly, I was worried.

"You're amazing," he said. "You're the last person I'd expect to go postal."

"Come on, it wasn't that bad." I hadn't shot or killed anyone. There wasn't even any blood that I could see.

"Given who you are, it was. And I love it." He shook his head admiringly. "We don't need a bodyguard, we have you."

"You're mocking me."

"No way. I'm proud of you." He got up to give me a warm hug, but there was a hard edge to his voice that troubled me. Did I *want* him to be proud of me, did I want him to relish my stepping over the line? Where were we headed?

Sitting next to me, Stefan made me retell the whole story of my "fight." What was I, Othello home from the wars? But I complied, because it made him happy and the last few days had been beyond hellish for him. And I was relieved to see that he was no longer shell-shocked— or at least not right then. Why not enjoy it—who knew how long this would last?

"I wish I'd been there," he said.

"To watch?"

"To finish him off."

I waited for him to chuckle or somehow indicate he was kidding, but his face was now set and grim, and his eyes distant.

"I thought you were detached from Stone, you'd gone all Zen and Let it Be."

Stefan shrugged. "I thought so, too. But man, the picture of him practically pissing his skinny jeans—"

"I didn't say that."

"You didn't have to. People like that are weasels, they're cowards, they're scum. They're like that pathetic car salesman in *True Lies* who pretends to be a spy so he can get laid, but ends up freaking out when he meets a real spy."

I wanted to tell him to chill, but who was I to get all directive? I'd said worse things about Stone. Besides, I was the one who'd hurt him.

Stefan jumped to his feet. "Let's go out and celebrate."

"Aren't you worried about running into people from the writing workshop, the organizers? They'll be angry you said no to being part of it, but you're here in town."

"Fuck 'em," he snapped.

It wasn't Shakespeare, but it fit. We took a soothing fifteen-minute walk over to the Jamesport Brewing Company, a big, relaxed, high-ceilinged bistro-ish restaurant off the main drag that was always crowded and always friendly. The door was enormously heavy and shrieked when you opened it, but the food inside was great. They gave us our favorite, curtained four-person alcove table where we had privacy to talk, and to do all the people watching we wanted to. Stefan was as ravenous as if he'd run a marathon in record time, a race he'd trained long and hard for, denying himself all his favorite food and drink. He ordered pecan-crusted perch and I watched him chow down, wondering if there wasn't something manic about the way he gobbled each mouthful.

"Aren't you hungry?" he pressed.

I shook my head and took a sip of my Amstel Light. I'd ordered their cheese ale soup, but hadn't eaten much. I'd become anxious each time the door opened, expecting police to come and drag me off for assaulting Stone. I imagined the headlines, because there was no way a story like that wouldn't transfix a little town like Ludington.

"What if I'm wrong?" I asked. "What if it isn't Stone who's targeting us, or orchestrating it, or involved in any way at all?"

Before Stefan could answer, he muttered, "Look who's here," and I turned to see Stone weaving from the bar toward us, limping slightly. He was all in black now, and looked shifty.

"You know," he said in an undertone when he reached us, "I once asked Christopher Hitchens why he never wrote anything about your memoir."

I had no idea Stone was friends with the late atheist author of *God Is Not Great*.

Stone leaned toward us, "He said it wasn't worth his time because Stefan was so obviously deluded, anyone with sense would see the desperation."

Stefan didn't even look up from his fish, and I expected him to explode, tip over the table and wrestle Stone to the ground. Or maybe that's what *I* wanted to do. The people at tables closest to us, sensing the confrontation, had stopped talking, but Stefan just kept eating.

"I'm not done with you," Stone said flatly and headed off.

When he was out of sight and presumably out the door, Stefan looked up at me and winked. He was actually ebullient. "That was supposed to flatten me? Hitchens was a great writer, I loved his essays. But I didn't write my memoir for him, so who cares what he said to Stone?"

"If he even said anything."

"Right. Too bad Hitchens *didn't* attack me, though, if the story's true. We could have sold twice as many books."

Stefan was right. Controversy, even the fake kind, was great PR for a book.

"Nick, have the rest of my fries, they're still warm."

I finished them, marveling at how unpredictable life with an author could be. Writers can be so thin-skinned, even a compliment phrased in the wrong way can feel like an insult to them—but then a bad review can unexpectedly make a writer laugh. Or a review he *didn't* get. How crazy was that?

"Stone wasn't kidding when he threatened you," I said, convinced once again that Stone was our man.

Stefan nodded. "His eyes," he said. And now his face dimmed. "Did you see them? Cold. Hard. He was *not* kidding, you're right. Maybe you got the better of him in the parking lot, but it won't end there."

"Why do you think he didn't report me to the police?"

Stefan shrugged. "It gives him an edge, or he thinks so, anyway." Then, speaking so softly that I might have missed it if I'd turned away, Stefan said without looking at me, "If I had the chance to kill him right now, right here in town, and get away with it, I'd do it."

11

Sunday morning, we had breakfast at our favorite place, Sophie's Lakeside Café, another easy walk from the condo. The bacon was crisp, the omelets were runny the way we liked them, the coffee strong and continuous. I loved everything about this neighborhood hangout: the nautical wallpaper border; the lighthouse prints and vintage photos of the harbor; the nets, wheels, and wooden anchors hanging on the walls; the captain's hat the elderly cashier wore at a comic angle; the paper table mats crammed with tiny local ads. The waitresses were cheerful and chatty; but then so were all the regulars who talked about boats and barns and cottages and grandchildren, and repeated old jokes to an appreciative audience. We were newcomers, of course, and regulars smiled at us genially enough, but the waitresses knew our names, commented on whether we were early or late compared to our usual arrival time, and made us feel at home.

I don't think my Belgian-born parents would have understood the charm of Sophie's. My mother and father didn't like servers to converse with them about anything but food, and the loose command of grammar you heard there would have appalled my proper mother and father: "them" instead of "those," "come" instead of "came." For me, it was all part of the atmosphere and blessedly far away from the pretentiousness of academia. And in a world of hyper-standardization, this café reminded me of an independent bookstore, relaxed, quirky, an outpost of individuality.

When we got home and were idly wondering what we'd do that day, my phone rang, and I panicked when I saw the caller ID: *Binnie.*

I shouted into the phone, "Something happened to Marco!"

"No, no, he's fine," Binnie assured me, but her voice was wavering.

"Then what?" I put her on speaker phone and set the phone on the counter as if to maintain a safer distance from the bad news, whatever it was.

"Marco didn't want to play with any of the dog toys I had, so since I had your key for emergencies, I went over to your house to bring back some of his, because puppies deserve the best, right? And, well, I think there was some kind of burglary there—"

Stefan and I both stared at the iPhone as if it were radioactive.

"There was a broken laptop on the floor in the foyer, and I was sure neither one of you would have left a mess like that, so I called the police right away. I told them I was a neighbor with your key and you were out of town, and they're sending someone over to investigate."

"We'll leave as soon as we can."

"Good! They want to talk to me, of course, but they need to talk to you, too. So it's good that you're coming home as soon as you can . . ." Binnie sounded really rattled by her discovery; she wasn't one to mindlessly repeat things you said.

I asked her how long ago she'd called the police. "Five minutes," she said. "Not more. Or much more."

Stefan said, "Binnie, are *you* all right?"

"Oh, yes, thanks. Thanks! I was startled, but I didn't look around, I just got the hell out of there. When I was back in my own house, I felt safe."

Lucky woman, I thought.

"Safer," she added tentatively. "And Marco was adorable—he could tell I was upset and he was very cuddly. Anyway, I'm going to wait outside for the police car now."

We thanked her, and I found myself apologizing for some reason, as if whatever happened had been my fault.

"Oh, go on with you," she said, affecting an Irish brogue. I think she was trying to make me at least smile. I was beyond that.

The air conditioning was turned up high, but I was sweating anyway as we packed quickly, checking and re-checking to make sure we weren't leaving anything behind, and that there was nothing in the fridge that would spoil while we were gone for however long it turned out to be. We didn't speak. As we got ourselves ready to leave, we might have been two spies methodically preparing for a dangerous mission.

Closing and locking the door of our condo, it hit me that someone could burglarize this place, too. But there was nothing I could do about that now.

We packed the car and drove off in silence.

I was angry, but only intellectually, as if I were studying a distant country on a map and observing its borders. I didn't *feel* anything, not really. I kept seeing horrific images of vandalism in my head, spray-painted walls, dishes and glasses shattered all over the kitchen floor, bedding cut apart by knives. But they were muffled in a way, because they were just visions. I didn't want to report that lurid private film, so I kept quiet. I suspected Stefan was living his own little hell, with images from the Holocaust of looted Jewish homes. If anything could trigger the trauma that had been passed on through his survivor parents, surely this news would do that as readily as the SWAT raid must have. And he was likely also thinking something close to what I was: "We have to deal with the Michiganapolis police again." It was a loathsome prospect.

Though rowdy teenagers sometimes took bats to metal mailboxes at night or even set the chunky plastic ones on fire, crime was low in our neighborhood and we did not have a burglar alarm system for our house. Years before, we'd had exterior photoelectric security lighting installed at each corner of the roof and over all the doors. Coming on at dusk, the lights cast a warm amber glow that softened their purpose: deterrence. The electrician had explained, "They won't stop anyone from breaking in, but it gives burglars a choice: your house or a house somewhere else in the neighborhood that doesn't have any lights at all."

I don't think it had never occurred to either of us that burglars would hit any house, during the day, but I realized it was a very canny choice—who would be around to see them?

I wanted to speed to Michiganapolis at ninety miles per hour, but when we got to the highway, I put on cruise control so we never went above seventy-five; getting stopped for a speeding ticket would have made me choke with frustration at the delay. I wanted to be home—and yet I dreaded being home. I felt as if I were some nineteenth-century character in a French or Russian novel forced to fight a duel over an insult he hadn't realized he'd uttered, and with a weapon he didn't know how to use. It was a nightmare, and I was doomed.

What made it all the worse was that Stefan and I had each retreated into our own doubts and fears; we were sitting in the same car, but we were isolated from each other. However big or small it was, we should have been sharing this new tragedy, somehow. But what was I supposed to say to bridge the silence, and why did I have to be the one to stitch up what had been torn apart? I felt dizzy and almost nauseous; the news from Binnie was triggering the same fear I'd felt the night when our home was invaded and our lives changed forever.

Binnie called halfway into our drive and we put her on the speaker.

"They sent one policeman," she said. "He checked the perimeter of the house, and didn't find any signs of a break-in."

Stefan said, "Huh," under his breath.

"What happened next?" I asked, feeling puzzled.

"He asked me if I had looked around inside and I said no, so he went in, his gun drawn. He checked the whole house. Nobody was inside, and the only evidence he found was the laptop in the foyer."

"That wasn't us," I assured her.

"I know, dear, and I told him so. You're such neat boys—look at your beautiful yard! He left his card for you to call him as soon as you get home. I know this is serious, but I was almost laughing when he gave it to me. He's got the oddest name, you'll never believe it: Kidd Pickenpack."

We thanked her and hung up. I felt oddly deflated. Our house had been invaded, somehow, and only one cop had been sent to investigate. Was that because we were still under suspicion somehow? Or was that standard for a possible burglary? My mouth felt very dry and I reached for the small bottle of water I'd stuck in the cup holder between me and Stefan. That seemed to shake Stefan out of his reverie, and he said, "Weird. Very weird."

"How did it happen? How did anybody break into the house?" I asked. "Without any signs of anything?"

"You read all those mysteries. Somebody must have picked the lock."

"Can you really do that?"

"Well, I can't," he said, with almost a trace of humor, but then he reverted to silence for another hour or more.

"It's definitely not Stone," Stefan finally blurted, as if his mind had been churning away every second since the last time he spoke. We were now about an hour from our exit.

"What? What do you mean? Why not him?"

"It's obvious. Stone could have gotten the SWAT team to hit us, however he did it. And maybe he was stalking you in town? But there's no way he could have burglarized our house when—" His words trailed off, and I knew why, and where he was going. He had realized that it didn't add up as soon as he started ruling Stone out because he'd been in Ludington when we were.

"Stone knew—or assumed—we were staying in Ludington at the condo," I said for Stefan, "and he could have driven to Michiganapolis late last night or even very early this morning."

"Yup."

"And driven back, and nobody at the writing workshop would know. Whatever Stone did at the house, he wanted to show us that he could, he wanted to keep us off-balance."

"I think it's working," Stefan said flatly, and we didn't say anything else until our exit, when I called Binnie to say we were almost home. We had to slow down first to thirty miles per hour, then twenty-five. It felt like crawling across glass as we wound so slowly through the mini-malls, gas stations, industrial buildings to the newer suburbs with big houses and small trees, past the edges of the university that was a universe of its own, to our own quiet neighborhood whose houses had been built before World War II and whose towering maples and oaks were older still. The transitions usually made us calmer. As a friend had said, Michiganapolis was a nice place to leave, but an even better place to live. You could get to Chicago, Toronto, Detroit, New York very easily— but it was soothing to return.

Not today. Our street felt almost toxic to me, the cars parked in driveways, the well-tended lawns, the rose bushes, summer clusters of Foxglove, coneflowers and delphinium, and the mounds of variegated hosta everywhere seemed ominous, portentous. Our house had been raided just a few days ago; I had been threatened while walking Marco; we'd gotten threatening phone calls at home and on campus; and now we'd been the target of a burglar. Or burglars. Why not more than one? Why not a whole team? It was all starting to run together like some kind of whirlpool of misfortune and I couldn't see myself breaking free.

86

Pulling into our driveway, I felt as crazed as if I were an American official besieged in one of our Middle Eastern embassies by a chanting mob. I had never had a migraine before in my life, and wondered if that's what I was experiencing now. I felt dizzy, had a terrible taste in my mouth as if I were close to vomiting, and my forehead throbbed.

Wordlessly, we parked in the garage, took out our bags, let ourselves into the kitchen from the side door. There was also a back door to the kitchen which led to the fenced backyard and *looked* secure. But the room suddenly felt vulnerable to me, more vulnerable even than our sun room which opened onto the large brick patio with its Viking grill and suite of outdoor furniture. Two doors, I thought, two ways to get in. Two weak spots.

"We have to get an alarm system," I said, putting down the Ralph Lauren leather duffel bag Stefan had bought me after sales of his memoir soared.

"Could we check the house first?" Stefan was carefully surveying the kitchen for signs of damage. When we'd had it remodeled it had seemed so solid and beautiful, now it struck me as just an empty gleaming shell.

"Whoa! You're saying we don't *need* one? What is wrong with you?"

"There's nothing wrong with me, and you don't have to yell. I'm standing right here."

"I'm not yelling!" Of course I was, and I knew it, but I was feeling panicky. If at that moment he'd tried to quiet me down any further, I would have exploded, but he wisely backed off and continued making a circuit of the kitchen, his Prada duffel still in his right hand. He opened drawers, cupboards, and the fridge.

I felt oddly as if I were an intruder in my own home. Stefan put his bag down and we left the kitchen. We found the broken laptop in the granite-floored foyer just as Binnie had said. It was the small Sony Vaio we used in the kitchen and the case was webbed with cracks. To my eyes, it looked more as if it had been dropped, rather than deliberately smashed: it was cracked and maybe even chipped, but not shattered.

"I don't think we should mess with it until we talk to the cop."

Just then, the doorbell rang, and we skirted the laptop to let Binnie in. She gave each of us a big hug, surprisingly big given how petite she was. "They'll get the swine that did this," she said. "I'm sure they will."

"Marco?" I asked.

"I thought I'd wait till you were done cleaning up, and talking to the police, before bringing him over. Is that okay? It seemed calmer for everybody."

"Very okay," I said, admiring her clear thinking. It was my turn to give her a hug, and she left. I studied the business card. His name really *was* Kidd Pickenpack. I read aloud the Michiganapolis police motto: "Preserve, Protect, Defend."

"Isn't that what the president swears to do for the Constitution when he takes his oath?" Stefan asked, frowning.

"I think it is."

I held the card out to him. "Do you want to call?"

He shook his head vigorously, as if to ward off some spell or curse, and backed away from the small white piece of card stock. "You call, I'll look around."

Stefan headed to his study, and I took out my phone. I got right through, explained who I was, and Officer Pickenpack said, "Ten minutes." I said fine, and spent the time going through the living room, the dining room, the half bath, even the hall closet, looking for any trace of someone having been there, but this wasn't like Will Smith in *Enemy of the State* where everything in his Georgetown home had been trashed and covered with graffiti. It was almost creepier. Why break into our house and just grab a laptop and then drop it? Could the burglar have been startled by something?

Stefan and I met back in the kitchen, and as soon as we sat down, the doorbell rang. I waved my hand at him, "Your turn, babe." He went to bring in Officer Pickenpack.

I don't know what I expected, but it wasn't an obvious weightlifter, who was a blond, fortyish junior version of the Hulk. Officer Pickenpack's legs were so muscular, he almost waddled, and his biceps and triceps were so large his upper arms looked swollen. The black uniform was like sausage casing, and everything else about him was robotic, one-dimensional. His face was square and blank, like one of those Depression-era statues representing some ideal. I'd thought I might be intimidated and even upset to have a representative of the Michiganapolis police in our home, but he was so cartoonishly fit, I felt almost blank.

He stood near the kitchen island, apparently oblivious to the room and to us. He got right to the point after we introduced ourselves and said how long we'd lived here, and he sounded bored stupid.

"Is anything missing? Any valuables? Cash? Electronics? No safe broken into?"

We shook our heads, and I waited for him to take out a note pad, but he just stood there impassively.

"You've searched the house thoroughly? Okay. Have you seen any suspicious people in the neighborhood recently?"

I hesitated, but Stefan said, "No. Never."

Pickenpack blinked, registering something, perhaps.

"There were no signs of forcible entry," he noted. "Who else has a key?"

I told him that Binnie did. "She's the neighbor who called you and took your card. She wouldn't have done this."

"Right. Okay. Do you have any special concerns?"

Stefan stared at him, and I said, "Yes. Why aren't you taking what happened more seriously?"

I swear Pickenpack almost yawned. "Sir, this isn't very serious as a police matter. Nothing's been vandalized or stolen. Nobody's been hurt. You just had one laptop damaged."

I corrected him: "Broken."

"The case is cracked. Have you tried turning it on?"

"I didn't think we were allowed to touch it. And aren't you going to dust it for finger prints first?"

He finally showed some emotion. He smirked as if I'd just said something unbelievably stupid, and his voice took on a surly edge, where before it had been just flat. "People watch too much *CSI*. You know who probably got into your house? A high school kid. Maybe even a junior high schooler. On a dare. It happens all the time."

"Not to us."

"It happens all the time," he insisted.

"But there aren't any signs of somebody breaking in, so you're telling me a *teenager* picked one of our locks?"

He nodded dourly.

"But how is that even possible?"

"You'd be surprised at what they can do." That's when I noticed his wedding band, and I wondered if he was thinking of his own kids. Who'd be more likely to get into trouble than a cop's children?

"All right, then," he concluded. "Call us if anything else happens." He turned slowly and lumbered out to the front door, Stefan following. I heard Stefan thank the officer and let him out.

"You thanked him?" I asked, when Stefan returned with the laptop and set it gingerly on the table. I started putting up a pot of coffee. "You really thanked him? For what? For not giving a shit? He was barely here ten minutes, and I bet he won't even file a police report."

"Probably not." Stefan shrugged, and it made me want to embroil him in one of those searing arguments that leave you exhausted, but purged. Except I knew I wasn't mad at *him*, but at the twister that had torn through our lives and left us damaged and lost. Twice now in less than a week, the police had been in our house. That was humiliating, and I was on the verge of losing it with Stefan when the doorbell rang. All I could think of was the satirist Dorothy Parker's sour reaction in similar situations: "What fresh hell is this?"

But then Stefan said, "Marco's back," and we both rushed to the door. Binnie handed off the leash as he jumped up around us, delirious with joy, and she said, "You boys need a pot roast—let's talk about when some other time," and she departed. As soon as we let Marco off his leash, instead of heading for the kitchen to his water bowl, he bounded upstairs.

Stefan squinted at me as if to say, "Did you see what I saw?"

"He's never done that before," I said, just as we could hear Marco barking frantically, the way he did when he'd see a strange dog in the neighborhood.

Voice low, I said, "There's someone in the bedroom."

Stefan rushed to get the poker from the fireplace; I grabbed the big emergency flashlight from the console table in the foyer, holding it like a club, and we surged up the stairs. We found Marco at the side of our cherry king sleigh bed, barking up at—at nothing.

"Did you check the closet, or under the bed before?"

"Of course not," he shot, while Marco growled and tried to climb up the side of the bed.

"What do you mean 'Of course not'? How does that make any sense?"

Stefan sighed and got on his knees to check under the bed, and I shut up and gingerly opened the closet, but it was clear Marco was being driven mad by the bed itself. We moved closer, and realized something smelled awful, but we couldn't see anything. Stefan started stripping away the pillows of all sizes, tossing them to the floor. Then he pulled back the blue and gold brocade duvet. The smell was awful now, something oily and noxious, like pond scum, or decayed, rotten food. Marco was practically leaping straight up into the air, trying to get at whatever was responsible for the stench. Stefan set down the poker and yanked back the sheets.

Lying in the middle of the bed was squashed and malodorous roadkill. We both leaped back in disgust from the pink and gray mess that was some unrecognizable animal.

"Fuck! Fuck! Fuck!" he shouted, and I thought he would go berserk, grab the poker, and destroy the entire room. Paralyzed, revulsed, I stared as he frantically balled up the sheet with the horrible mess at its center, holding the bulky package as far away from himself as possible while Marco danced around as if it were some new intriguing game. Cursing when it got stuck, he yanked off the mattress pad, wrapped it around the sheet inside and rushed downstairs.

"Where are you going?" I called.

I followed him and found him behind the garage, thrusting the mattress pad and sheet into a yard waste bag and then into the large green plastic trash cart. "Get the quilt," he ordered. "And all the pillows!" Marco was out there now, sitting down, head cocked, watching him, curious. I trooped upstairs, grabbed the rest of the beautiful Dian Austin bed linens, and dragged the lot downstairs. Stefan stuffed the rest of it into the trash cart, and slammed the lid shut, breathing hard, face twisted and red.

I grabbed a can of Lysol from the pantry, headed reluctantly up to the room that our stalker had polluted as badly as the police had violated the whole house. But before I did anything, I opened every drawer, checked every shelf in the closet for more gruesome evidence that we had been targeted by a very sick mind. I didn't find anything, but wondered if there was a trap somewhere, waiting to be sprung on us, that might take us days to find.

Luckily, the dead critter, whatever it was, had not stained the mattress itself because the mattress pad had a waterproof backing. I sprayed the bed liberally, but what I really wanted was a flamethrower to burn the mattress and bed to ash, sweep it all up and pretend it had never been there. The room reeked of Lysol when I was done. We would have to sleep in the guestroom till it wore off. Maybe every night from now on. It was large enough, and the bed there was fairly new.

"We're not safe anymore," Stefan said behind me, from the top of the stairs. "We'll never be safe." And he sat down on the top step, covered his face with his hands and howled his despair.

12

Feeling shaky, I left him alone, went down to the kitchen, called Marco and sat outside on the patio, trying to relax and enjoy the garden. Marco sat by my feet and I closed my eyes, leaned back in the zero gravity recliner I'd come to rely on for stress management. I listened to the breeze stirring the leaves high above us. You couldn't hear much traffic where we lived, but it was a noisy day in the trees and hedges: chickadees, mourning doves, cardinals, finches, and sparrows. I welcomed the soft cacophony in our half acre of heaven.

But though I was physically comfortable, my mind was tormented by the gross scene of discovering *roadkill* in our bed, and the dread of further outrages. I kept coming back to the fear that whoever was behind all this had planted subtler little bombs in other rooms. I couldn't even imagine what they could be, but sensed their menace. I was starting to feel as if I were living in a haunted house. The ordinary had turned threatening, even malevolent.

Marco suddenly bolted for the far side of the yard and I hurried after him. I wasn't in the mood to clean up after him if he caught a rabbit; he thankfully didn't chew on them, just broke their necks, but sometimes there was blood. Luckily, when I caught up to him, he was just sniffing idly along the fence; whatever he'd seen or thought he'd seen was gone. Mr. Kurtz was digging on the other side (of course!), and now he stood up and glared at me, looking like the farmer in Grant Wood's *American Gothic*.

"What the hell is going on at your place? The police are there every single day," he snarled. "I don't like it. Nobody likes it. People like you don't belong here. This is a *decent* neighborhood."

I was gobsmacked, since he almost never spoke to me or Stefan.

"What the hell are you doing over there, running some kind of meth lab?" he asked, and since the fence was only four feet high, I could have easily reached across and belted him. But I turned, clapped my hands for Marco, who followed me back inside.

"My son-in-law is a cop!" he called. As if that meant anything.

In the kitchen I felt as angry and frustrated as a bullied, fat adolescent, and I wanted to stuff my face and stuff down every last feeling, but I couldn't figure out what to eat, so I just stood there, helpless. And then the image of the polluted bed upstairs triggered another image: a larger bed in a far more magnificent room. From a movie: *The Godfather.* There was a studio executive in that film who didn't want to give an Italian singer a big part, so the singer asked the Godfather for help, and the exec was punished by finding the head of his prize horse in his king-size bed.

Lucky Bitterman, I thought. He was steeped in films; someone like that would be bound to recreate moments from movies, whether he was conscious of it or not. No, roadkill wasn't a horse's head, but then Michiganapolis wasn't Hollywood, either. Stone had filled my mind ever since I'd discovered he was in Michigan, but the first person I'd suspected was Lucky, and now he loomed larger than ever. It was time to do something about him, to find out if he was persecuting us, and to make him stop if he was.

As if someone were tugging at my shoulder, I remembered Officer Pickenpack telling us to call if anything else happened. But calling him at this moment seemed pointless. I pictured myself facing that big blank face of his again, imagined his suspicious questions. Wouldn't he wonder why we hadn't found the mess upstairs sooner? And what would he do about this, given how trivial our situation seemed to him? Besides, even if he did return to investigate the room and the mess in our trash cart, anybody smart enough to pick our lock wouldn't have left clues to their identity.

But there was another reason for my reluctance: I felt ashamed. It was the shame of someone being victimized who feels doubly exposed talking about the violation. None of this was my fault, and yet the escalation was making me feel more and more that I wanted to hide. If one set of neighbors was angry at us, what about everyone else on our street aside from Binnie and Vanessa? Were we going to be pariahs? Berated while out for a walk? Shunned at local stores and movie theaters? Avoided at neighborhood association meetings?

The next morning, Stefan wandered into the kitchen, looking as pale and listless as the knight in Keats's "La Belle Dame sans Merci." Not feeling much like eating, I told him I was going to campus to check my mail, and he barely registered what I said. Good. Because he would have reminded me that there wasn't much mail in the summer months.

At Parker Hall, I stopped on the second floor for my mail, still disoriented by how cheaply done the renovations were here. The permanent faculty a floor above might hate their little cubicles, but at least they didn't look this flimsy. There also wasn't any welcome desk on this floor or anyone to ask for what you needed, just brooding silence and a smog of resentment. It was the kind of grim, characterless environment that could drain anyone's hope and enthusiasm, and I disliked being on this floor any longer than necessary.

Stepping off the elevator one floor above moments later after I'd sorted the handful of mail I'd received, I felt again how cold and impersonal the environment was, down to the new strange "ding" of the elevator. I said hello to Estella, our tattooed and pierced greeter, as I was beginning to think of her. Today she was actually wearing a spikey crimson wig, and she sported glittery red and white fingernails. I flinched when the flashing sign hanging above her welcomed me, hoped I was having a good summer, and told me the temperature outside.

The department chair, Juno Dromgoole, stepped briskly out of her office far off to the right and beckoned me with her raised index and middle fingers. "Nick? A word, please." I swear I'd seen that gesture on some TV show where it was used by an imperious boss.

I threaded my way around the outside of the mass of cubicles to answer what was clearly a summons, not an invitation. Since being elevated to the position of chair, Juno had changed her style as dramatically as our office space had been changed. She was now frigid and dictatorial. She still wore Manolo Blahnik or Badgley Mischka shoes, but her leopard print skirts were gone, ditto the clouds of expensive, attention-getting perfume. She almost always wore conservatively cut suits, looking like Demi Moore in *Margin Call*: controlled, powerful, remote. Stefan and I had speculated that just this small taste of authority had made her hungry to rise much higher at SUM.

Weirdly, her office was decorated with blue-gray French Provincial furniture and Watteau prints, as if to take the edge off her iciness. I sat opposite her desk in a pretty but very uncomfortable chair (the latter was probably deliberate). She closed the door and sat down behind her curlicued desk, tented her hands together under her chin, surveying me. I didn't squirm, because I remembered all the rowdy times we'd had together years before, and I remembered her swimming in the pool at our health club in a sexy gold one-piece that could turn anyone on. It wasn't the same as the public speaking tip to imagine your audience naked so as to feel less intimidated, but close enough.

I was past intimidation by administrators, anyway. In fact, I was tempted to mimic her pose and fold my hands as she was doing, but decided not to be inflammatory. Studying her in turn, I realized that since the last time I'd seen her in the spring, she'd had one of those plastic surgery makeovers like Madonna and other celebrities, the kind that's partly done from the inside of the mouth and turns your face heart-shaped, with wider eyes, more prominent cheekbones, and a pointier chin. It was a bit creepy because it looked mass-produced.

"You seem to have a problem with the police," she said flatly.

"Do I?"

"The police have been to your house. What kind of example is that to set for students, and how does that make our department look?"

"The students aren't here, or most of them, and I haven't done anything."

"But it *looks* bad," she insisted, mouth rigid. "I'm telling you this not as your chair, but as your friend."

Did department chairs *have* friends? Allies, maybe—at the most.

"Bullerschmidt told you, didn't he?" I asked. Who else could it have been?

"I won't be interrogated about my contacts with anyone."

Well, that was as good as a confession, and I must have rattled her a bit because she went on to say, "Really, Nick, twice in one week is—"

"What do you mean *twice*?"

She flushed under all that makeup and blush.

"We had a break-in yesterday and you know already? How is that even possible? Wait, don't tell me, Bullerschmidt again. Unless you have your *own* spies."

She folded her arms and glared at me, clearly annoyed at having revealed too much. "I need to know what my faculty are doing at all times. They represent the department, and the university. They represent *me*."

It amazed me that the woman I used to know—who'd been so edgy, contentious, foul-mouthed, a real gadfly—had turned into such a dictatorial robot. Could she really believe that line of bullshit? And how could she not even ask if I was okay, if I needed help? I wasn't a person to her anymore, not even a colleague. I was a PR problem. If she could press a delete key on her laptop and make me disappear, I'm sure she would have done that. I briefly thought of appealing to her better side, but I doubted anything could penetrate that new carapace of inhuman efficiency.

Then something hit me, something disturbing. It hadn't felt like pure coincidence that I got off the elevator and she called me to her office. She had been *waiting* for me, I was sure of it.

"When they remodeled last summer, did they install surveillance cameras? Did you know I was already in the building?"

"I'm not at liberty to discuss campus security."

"Take the stick out of your butt and tell me the truth." It was the kind of thing she might have said in the old days, and I swear she almost smiled. Well, her lips twitched.

"It's important for all of us to be safe," she said primly. "Whatever it takes."

"Does the faculty know? Is this even public?"

"Is what public? I haven't told you anything."

She was born to be an administrator; she'd gone into cover-your-ass mode as quickly as a reef polyp retreating into its tiny coral fortress.

"And you should think twice before spreading unfounded rumors," she added.

"Where are they? The cameras, I mean. The elevators? The lobby downstairs? The mail room? *Everywhere?*"

She was rigid and unsmiling. "I want to warn you, Nick, that you're in enough trouble already."

"Why? I told you: I haven't done anything."

"If you get arrested, what happens to the Nick Hoffman Fellowship? How many authors will want to associate themselves with your name then?"

I didn't know what she meant about being arrested, but it unnerved me. $25,000 was a great honorarium, but if it came with bad publicity, people might think twice about applying.

"You can't bully me, Juno," I said.

She leaned her head back and looked down her nose at me. "Nobody dreamed we could ever get rid of Alberta, and she's gone now, isn't she?"

Alberta Starr had been one of EAR's least popular professors, both with students and colleagues. Cold, arrogant, insufferable, she had taught at SUM for three decades, but hadn't published in her field for the last twenty years. Starr held a Guggenheim Fellowship early in her career and acted as if that made her royalty; but once she'd been granted tenure, she just coasted. Starr didn't have an ounce of collegiality, and showed no desire to mentor or even instruct students. She avoided department meetings, and when she did come, she insulted people directly or obliquely, and always left before the meetings were over. Even worse, she badmouthed other faculty to students, making them feel they were privileged to hear the gossip, but the effect was to poison their experiences in those professors' classrooms. Starr's departure had been a jubilee for EAR; even in our notoriously snarky department, the woman was exceptional for malice and narcissism.

I stared at her. "Starr was ill, wasn't she? That's why she retired in the middle of last fall and you had to get people to cover her classes."

"Oh, yes, she was unwell. True enough," Juno said smugly. "But I got rid of her myself." Juno didn't explain how she had made Starr an offer she couldn't refuse, and I didn't challenge her.

"There's something else," Juno said, and if anything, she looked harder and colder. "I understand that Stefan is still defying the administration about that suicide book."

"Why are you talking to *me* about it? Talk to him."

"Because I think you might be a bit more reasonable."

I presumed that meant weak, and I felt insulted.

"Nick, a book like that could cause more damage than you realize. What if it sparked copycat suicides at the university?"

I hesitated, because the question had occurred to me, too, but I hadn't brought it up with Stefan because I had never tried to talk him out of writing *any* book.

"So what do you want me to do?" I asked, trying to sound defiant, but I suspect I came across as abject and apologetic.

Juno relaxed, looking almost reasonable. "Tell him that giving up the book would be a tremendous service to SUM. And publishing it would be something he'd seriously regret. Something you would *both* regret."

"What do you mean?"

Juno buzzed her secretary. "We're done here, Nick."

I wasn't feeling cocky anymore, and I left with a whole new miasma of paranoia settling over me like volcanic ash. First the dean had threatened Stefan and me, and now my chair was also acting the heavy.

But that wasn't the only reason I felt dirty and burdened. The remodeling from last summer wasn't just egregiously impersonal—it was also intrusive if there was secret surveillance going on. But who was monitoring all of this, and why?

I felt dizzy with all this anxious speculation. Juno had threatened the viability of the Nick Hoffman Fellowship—was somebody trying to wrest it away from me? That was impossible, surely? The conditions were ironclad: if I wasn't involved, the money disappeared from SUM. My mind reeled. What if everything that had been happening to Stefan and me was somehow connected to a larger development at the university? The whole country was security-crazed—had the sickness infected SUM, too?

I crossed the length of the floor to my office on the other side of the building, wondering how many people—if any—were hunched in their cubicles, trying to maintain some shred of privacy and concentration. Talk about surveillance—you could be watched and studied by anyone in there, and you wouldn't even know it.

"Honey, you don't look so good," Celine said as I walked through her office to mine.

She, of course, looked great as always in sandals, flowing purple cotton skirt and matching sleeveless top.

"Sit down and close the doors," I said. "All of them."

Celine gave me an odd look, but did what I asked her to, and then joined me. I told her the entire story of the last few days, all of it, and her face mirrored almost everything I'd been feeling. It was scary to see how affected she was, because it deepened the terror I'd been experiencing, but it also felt cathartic. I wasn't quite as alone anymore. When I was done, Celine shook her head and said, "Un-be-liev-able. I am so sorry this is happening to you."

"Do you think I'm wrong not to report my suspicions to the police?"

"I wouldn't want the Gestapo in my house, either." She added a quick "Sorry!"—but I wasn't offended. She wasn't a politician invoking the Nazis to score political points.

And then she glanced around the office, as if wondering if it was bugged. The thought hadn't occurred to me, but if there were surveillance cameras in the building, why not listening devices as well? The university was a public institution, but it was increasingly being run like a dictatorship. There was no real oversight of the president and the provost; the faculty senate was powerless; and money and prestige were the driving forces on campus. Or at least they had been; now "security" had been added to the mix.

"Do you have friends in other departments?" I asked. "Have you heard them talking about surveillance?"

Celine hesitated. "Well, I did just hear a rumor. There's some kind of high-level committee that's been formed, a secret committee, and they're going to monitor the campus for threats 24/7."

"Terrorist threats?"

She shook her head. "No, like Virginia Tech and other schools, where somebody goes nuts with a gun. They'll be expecting everyone on campus to report threatening behavior, and the reports can be anonymous. And they'll be able to investigate anyone, even staff and professors, read their emails, tap their phones, whatever it takes, and then maybe even arrest them or have them committed before they've done anything."

"That's insane."

"That's SUM, Nick. And their name is hinky, too: JSOC, Joint Security On Campus. Sounds almost like the military, doesn't it?"

I shrugged. The name struck me as typical: a benign-sounding title for something nefarious. And if what Celine had told me was true, that probably meant the reality was much worse. No wonder Juno had mentioned arrest.

"Can you find out more?" I asked. "Like who's *on* this committee?"

Celine nodded. "Sure. But let me get something straight. Juno threatened you about the fellowship? There's nothing she can do about that. It's set up as a trust."

"But if the university wanted to break the trust and go to court, I couldn't stop them, could I?"

Celine shrugged. "Let me ask my friend in the Law School what she can find out."

"Thanks! Now, tell me if you think I'm nuts to suspect Lucky Bitterman of masterminding what's been going on."

"Oh no, he could do it. He's a lowlife and he hates you. Well, he hates everyone. But he hates you especially. You *and* Stefan. In my opinion, it's because he's a closet case."

"A reaction formation," I suggested.

"Yes, something like that. And the guy's a volcano, sooner or later he has to explode. I'm surprised it hasn't happened already."

"Can you get me his address?"

Celine frowned. "You're not going over there to rough him up, are you?"

"Of course not! This is for information only. I want to see what kind of car he's driving."

She popped into her office for the department address book, returned to read off Lucky's, and I thanked her for listening.

"Be careful," she warned.

Downstairs in the parking lot, I noticed a white panel truck with darkened windows, like the kind you see in thrillers. It was off by itself, and had no logo on the side. It was not remotely the kind of vehicle faculty members drove. Was a security team huddled there, listening in on everyone inside Parker Hall?

13

Lucky's neighborhood was very different from ours, studded with rambling, run-down Tudor homes that housed fraternities. The lawns were drier, the trees were newer, and the single family houses were all small and undistinguished-looking, as if trying to avoid attention. This neighborhood had to be pretty noisy on weekends, given all the students, which certainly wouldn't have made Lucky any nicer.

I turned onto his street, noting which side the even numbers were on, and just then Lucky loped by in black and blue running gear, looking far more athletic than I would have guessed he was from having seen him around the department. His quads were enormous and even when he stopped in front of a white Cape Cod with a privet hedge and variegated spirea out front, he looked powerful. I slowed down, watched him let himself in the front door. All the curtains were drawn and I didn't think he saw me. His garage door was closed, and looking at the modest house, I couldn't imagine him driving a car that started at $45,000 and could go almost twenty thousand higher when fully loaded.

But then why not? He could be a car nut or status-hungry and love expensive cars more than anything else. I had to know for sure what he drove, and couldn't figure out how. Not thinking very clearly, I took several right turns and found myself cruising down his street again. This time when I passed his house, the curtains were open on a picture window and he was staring out at me, shirtless now, glaring, looking angry and tough. Shit! He had seen me when he ran by. Now *I* was the one who could be accused of stalking. I had truly fallen down the rabbit hole.

I sped off, deciding to confer with Stefan and see if he could help me come up with a plan. I drove homeward pondering how my whole life had changed in a few harrowing days, as completely as if we'd survived a bombing or one of us had been diagnosed with terminal cancer. The vernal beauties of our street left me untouched as I pulled up to our house and parked in the driveway. For the first time since moving in, I imagined what it might be like to leave this gorgeous house. Despite my bluster with Bullerschmidt and Juno Dromgoole, I felt very tentative about my position, and apprehensive about my ability to remain at SUM. It was a far from perfect work environment, but Stefan and I had both fallen in love with Michigan and finding another university where both of us could teach would be very hard, maybe impossible.

I let myself in and looked around for Marco, who usually greeted me in the foyer when I used the front door. I called his name and heard a faint whine. I followed that sound upstairs to the guest room where Stefan was sprawled on the bed, face down. The beige quilt was rolled back and his right arm hung down over the side, fingers almost touching the carpet. His mouth gaped, and he was breathing so deeply I could hear it. It was almost snoring, and sounded very strange. Marco sat near his hand, sniffing it and moaning. Stefan looked drunk and passed out, but he couldn't have gotten plastered in the time I'd been gone, could he?

"Stefan, I'm home."

Marco briefly turned to eye me, but shifted his attention back to Stefan, and moaned more loudly. He sounded desolate. I walked to the bed and shook Stefan's arm, but he didn't stir. Was he ill? I crouched down next to him, turned his head and felt his forehead—normal. And then I saw a brown plastic pill bottle on the lamp table standing on top of a book about the painter Tamara de Lempicka. The pill bottle was open and empty. I picked it up to read the label. Valium.

I slapped him. "Bastard! Don't you fucking kill yourself and leave me alone!"

Marco shot out of the room, and Stefan groaned. I took out my phone to dial 911, already picturing the new scandal of an ambulance pulling up outside our door, and hesitated. Stefan mumbled, "What are you doing?" He squinted at me and struggled to sit up.

"Calling 911 to get your stomach pumped!"

"Wha—What for? What are you talking about?" He blinked at me groggily, as if he couldn't focus well.

"How many did you take? How many Valium did you take?"

Now he was waking up, and he was angry. He felt his reddened cheek. "Did you slap me? You slapped me. I can't believe it."

"I can't believe you'd try to OD on Valium!"

He used his right arm to push himself up and sat very straight, like a drunk trying to prove he was sober. Enunciating his words overdistinctly, he said, "I took one to calm down, and it didn't help. So I took two more."

"That's fifteen milligrams."

"So? I wasn't going anywhere. I needed oblivion."

It was a lot of Valium, more than either of us ever took at a time, but it wasn't an overdose. I sank into the thick armchair opposite him and hung my head, ashamed at having panicked and slapped him. I mumbled some sort of apology, and didn't say anything about picturing Father Ryan giving him the last rites.

"Sometimes, Nick, you can be a real idiot."

"At least it's only sometimes," I said, and looked up at him, hoping he would be amused.

He tried to chuckle, but was still too woozy to make it work. Marco crept back into the room, sensed all was well, and then loped over to me, tail wagging, to get his neck scratched. He repeated the process with Stefan, who gingerly helped him onto the bed. Marco settled against a pillow and promptly fell asleep. As always, I envied that.

"You can put away your phone," Stefan said softly.

I looked down and saw that I was clutching it hard enough to draw blood if it'd had any sharp edges. I slid it into my jeans pocket.

"I came in here," he explained, "to try the room out, to see if it felt comfortable." We'd ordered everything in it—bed, chair, tables, lamps, linens—from Restoration Hardware the day after we'd seen a new catalogue, admiring the beige, black, and white blends of fabrics and the bed's high quilted headboard.

"Do you think we can ever go back across the hall, back to our bedroom?" I asked, looking around the guestroom I rarely went into. It had always seemed attractive to me before, but today, the room looked unlived in. Though I suppose if we slept there, eventually it would feel comfortable, wouldn't it?

"Nick, you really thought I would commit *suicide*? After what happened to my student?" Stefan was glaring at me, and I dreaded an argument. I was too worn out.

"I'm sorry, really sorry. But I couldn't wake you up, Marco was whining, and I saw the pill bottle. How was I supposed to know you only took three?"

"That's all that was in there, and did you see a suicide note? No. I'm a writer. I would never go without leaving a note."

"Oh. Good point." Now I felt truly abashed.

"Hey—that was a joke."

I couldn't take it in. As if my body had been frozen somehow in the few minutes I thought he had taken an overdose, I could now sense the blood pulsing too quickly in my veins and my face was flushed, my breathing raspy, and I felt as if I'd been running after something I couldn't catch. Or maybe running *from* something was a better way to put it.

Stefan read me perfectly, and said what I was thinking: "Things have been happening so fast, we haven't had any time to really process what's been going on."

"Even if we had the time, would it make a difference? I feel like I'm trapped on the roof of my house in a flood, and the water keeps rising."

He nodded. "I've been praying, trying to pray, but I can't concentrate, I can't get quiet enough inside."

I had never put much stock in prayer, but I sympathized because I knew it was important now to Stefan, who seemed surprisingly alert, given the Valium and the last few days of trauma.

"It must be dinner time," I said. "Let's eat something and try to clear our minds. We need to take control. Or at least try."

We found Marco in the kitchen waiting for his own dinner. I fed him his kibble while Stefan set the table and put some goulash in the microwave to defrost. I told him about Juno's claim to have axed Alberta Starr herself, which seemed even more extraordinary when I repeated the story, because what could she possibly have done to get rid of a tenured faculty member?

"Maybe she blackmailed Alberta?" Stefan suggested.

"How? With what?"

Then I told him about Juno's threats if he didn't stop writing *Fieldwork in the Land of Grief*.

"Nobody's going to keep me from finishing that book, not the dean, not Juno, not even you."

I protested: "Don't lump me with them."

"But you're not crazy about the book, admit it."

"I'm ambivalent. The whole thing is so raw, and look how much trouble it's causing us without even being published." I didn't want to continue, so I told him that Juno had implied EAR was under surveillance. Stefan went pale, whether from anger or fear, I don't know.

"Sex tapes," I said. "What if Alberta Starr was screwing a student in her office? Or doing drugs?"

Stefan thought that over and said, "The timing fits, if there *is* full surveillance at Parker Hall. The remodeling was finished last summer before the fall semester began."

"But that would mean everything I've said in my office to anyone has been recorded."

Once again, Stefan looked like Death eating a sandwich, and I felt queasy myself. I told him what Celine had said about the rumored secret committee, and if possible, he looked even more stunned, eyes glassy, mouth tight. "They're turning SUM into a police state," he muttered.

The doorbell rang. I made an effort not to curse or sigh, and went out to the door. Happily, it was Vanessa, brandishing a bottle of red wine. "Vino Nobile di Montepulciano 2007," she said. "I had a lot of this last summer in Tuscany. They'll tell you in wine stores it needs another year or two, but I think it's ready now."

"*I'm* ready now," I said. "Thanks!"

Vanessa was looking sleek and cool in a black leather skirt and matching sleeveless silk top. She had the arms of Linda Hamilton in the *Terminator* movies; I don't know why, but I found that as reassuring as her Brooklyn toughness.

I brought the bottle in to Stefan like a kid showing off his A for homework, "Look what Vanessa brought us."

Stefan grinned. "One of my favorites. *Our* favorites," he corrected.

Vanessa glanced from me to Stefan and back. "Good," she said. "You're still talking to each other."

"What do you mean?" I asked.

"I warned you. Legal trouble drives couples apart," she said. "I've seen it happen a lot. The stress and humiliation, the burden just gets to be too much."

I closed my mind to those possibilities of chaos infecting my relationship with Stefan. I brought out big wine glasses and opened the bottle. I didn't wait for the wine to breathe; instead, I poured us all generous portions and we toasted silently, clinking glasses by the kitchen island.

"Wow," I said. "This wine is *big*." It was round and full-bodied, with a terrific long finish. I thanked Vanessa again, and we invited her to join us for dinner and a strategy session.

"You're having goulash?" she said. "I love goulash! I'm only half-Italian, the other half is Hungarian."

"Like Stephanie Plum!" I said.

Vanessa frowned. "Who's that?"

"You know, the heroine in Janet Evanovich's mysteries?"

She shrugged, but then said, "Wait—the funny ones set in New Jersey? I've heard about them, but I don't typically read books like that. I'm more into biography and history." She turned to Stefan and asked, "Does he always see things in terms of books?"

"I think we both do. Occupational hazard." Stefan set another place at the table. It might have been too hot a day for any kind of stew, but the air conditioning kept the house pleasant, and I found just the *idea* of goulash very comforting. The wine didn't hurt, either. But before we started, Stefan handed Vanessa a check I didn't know he had written.

"We haven't had any time to talk about a retainer—is five thousand okay, or do you need more?" He looked at me, and I nodded my approval, wondering how I hadn't even thought of raising this question with Vanessa. She was a lawyer after all, not a social worker.

She nodded, and put the check in her skirt pocket. "I wanted to give you time to recover. And yes, five thousand is just fine for now." She spoke about money without embarrassment; I liked that. Marco liked her; he had fallen asleep under Vanessa's chair after finishing his kibble.

We ate and talked about the news in Michigan, climate change, the price of gas, and the culture shock of moving to Michiganapolis from the East Coast. We marveled at how people in-state tended to claim they had no accent, and how Michiganders didn't seem to travel much, even in the Midwest. It was a pleasant, stress-free conversation, and Vanessa deftly kept it that way until we had espresso.

"Now, fill me in," she said, crossing her arms, but the gesture wasn't like Juno's, cold and forbidding. Somehow it seemed to invite intimacy.

I complied with ease, and I could feel her taking mental notes as I walked her through the days since the night our home was invaded. She was clearly not the kind of person who interrupted her concentration by writing things down when she was focused and listening. That, too, reassured me.

When I was done, she asked for specifics about the parking lot incident in Ludington. "You have some exposure there," she said, "if he decides to sue you or involve the police, but the longer it goes, the better your chances. I'm guessing from how you described him that he wants to keep you off-balance, so he isn't going to report the encounter."

I thought that was a great choice of words, better than "incident" or anything else that suggested violence. I didn't mind the rhetorical camouflage.

"Did his car have a Michigan license plate?" she asked.

I felt like an idiot admitting that I didn't remember, but Vanessa wasn't perturbed. She probably had lots of clients come up short on more important details.

Stefan asked, "Do you think he's the one who's after us? Stone?"

Vanessa sighed, uncrossing her arms and folding her French-manicured nails. "I like both of them for your stalker, him and that Bitterman guy. But we need something more than suspicion."

"Can Lucky have me arrested for stalking?"

Vanessa laughed. "You drove by his house a coupla times? Puh-leeze. I'd like to see him try."

"Is there a way we can find out what kind of car Lucky drives? And check where Stone's car was rented or if it really was a rental?"

Vanessa leaned back and crossed her long legs. She was wearing glittery black Jimmy Choo pumps I'd seen in *Vanity Fair* not so long ago. "That's pretty simple," she said. "My firm employs a husband-and-wife PI team. I can have them find out in probably a day or two at most. They'll check with the secretary of state's office and the courts if they need to. Both of them used to be cops, and people do them favors all the time. It'll just go on your tab. Oh, and if you want, they can check on that white van you saw on campus, too, if you got the plate number. No? Okay, another time for that."

Before she could go on, I told her about the two threatening phone calls, and she mused, "Okay, maybe it's time to have your lines monitored. Let me think about it. Now, what about your department chair, that June—"

"Juno. Juno Dromgoole."

"Christ, what a name," Vanessa murmured.

"Why are you asking about her?"

Vanessa studied her nails for a moment, then looked back up at me. "She sounds pretty vengeful and determined."

"But we used to be friends, or something like friends." Then I added. "Before she was the chair."

"There you go—*used* to be. But now she's got power and she's abusing it. What if she's out to get you? I'm just thinking out loud here. I have friends in academia in New York and Boston. I know jobs are very tight now. What if she wants to get rid of one or both of you because she has friends she'd like to have hired in your place?"

Stefan and I exchanged a long, anxious look. Vanessa's chilling scenario was all too possible.

Vanessa went on: "She doesn't sound mentally stable to me, but she's functional, right? Maybe she and your dean could be in on this together . . . or she's just going rogue."

"There's something else," I said. "The administration isn't happy with us, well, with Stefan because of his new book. It's about a student of his who committed suicide."

"The one who hanged himself on campus?" she asked. "I was in Rome when that happened, but I did hear something about it."

"That's the guy," Stefan said quietly. "They want me to drop the book."

"Why? Are you blaming the school for his death? No? So there's nothing actionable in your book. And aren't you allowed to publish whatever you like?"

"Nobody at SUM is worried about infringing on academic freedom—they're as paranoid about bad PR as North Korea."

Vanessa nodded several times as if absorbing all the new information. "You aren't the most popular guys at SUM, are you? Right now, anyway. Do you know what she drives?"

"You mean Juno? It's a black Chrysler 300. She buys a new one every other year. She brags about it."

Vanessa closed her eyes as if picturing the car. "Doesn't that have a fat grill, kind of like the Cadillac XTS?"

"The Caddy has that little shield of theirs on the center of the grill."

"Right, but think about it. Is it possible you mixed up the two cars because you were distracted? Are you absolutely *positive* it wasn't a Chrysler following you in town?"

I wanted to say I was sure, but with everything that had been happening this past week, nothing seemed certain, especially since I now had to worry that the chair of my own department might have launched a vicious campaign to drive me from my job and my home.

14

We had espresso in the living room and it heartened me that Marco leapt onto the couch where Vanessa was sitting, cuddling against her as she stroked his back and head. Maybe I was naïve, but when he liked someone, I always trusted his instincts.

"Do you have dogs?" I asked.

"Not now, my hours are too crazy, but I grew up with them." It occurred to me that aside from having noted that she wasn't wearing a wedding ring, I knew nothing about her private life.

Vanessa set her cup down on the coffee table. "I need to ask some other questions that might feel awkward, and I want to remind you that everything you say to me is privileged, okay?"

We nodded, and I felt apprehensive. What more could she possibly need to know?

"Okay. Do you have any pending lawsuits or criminal charges? Are there any restraining orders against either of you? Any arrests of any kind?"

We both shook our heads.

"Good. Now, I'm your lawyer, I represent you, I defend you in court if need be, and I'm not here to judge. Everyone's human, lawyers know that best. So—is there anyone in your department you haven't mentioned who might be after you? Somebody you had an affair with, or made a pass at, for instance. You've been here, what, fifteen years? That's a long time. Or maybe someone made a pass at *you* and you turned them down, and now we're dealing with their frustration and revenge."

We both said "No" at the same time, and I added, "Absolutely not."

"Great. One more question. Is there anything you haven't told me that could have a bearing on what's been going on, anything at all? Think about it."

After a moment, I shook my head, and Stefan followed suit, but without even looking at him, I could tell from his hesitation and the slightly altered tone of his voice that he was lying, and it astonished me.

When I did glance his way I saw that he had uncrossed his legs, which was his "tell." Lying, he unconsciously tried to make himself seem more open and relaxed, but I'd seen this before. I made an effort to suppress what I was feeling, and hoped that if Vanessa did notice my distress, she would assume it was the general situation that was hitting me hard, not the specific question.

She wasn't done. "You told me you don't have a gun in the house, right? Well, you might want to think about getting one."

I was dumbfounded. "Why?"

"Honestly, I'm concerned for your safety. Too much has happened in less than a week, and it's escalating. Someone threatened to run you down, the break-in, the roadkill in your bed, the threatening phone calls . . ." She left the sentence unfinished as if she expected more, and soon.

"But we'd have to take a gun safety course, and you can't get a permit overnight."

Vanessa corrected me. "You can apply for a permit to purchase a handgun and get the background check done in twenty-four hours. And gun safety training is recommended, of course, but it's not required unless you're applying to carry a concealed weapon."

"Wow," I said, "they've sped it up since last time—" I stopped, but it was too late. I don't know why, but I had not wanted Vanessa to know I'd even thought of owning a gun a decade ago when I got assaulted at SUM.

Vanessa waited for my explanation.

"Back when Juno and I were friends, or whatever we were, we went gun shopping because of crazy stuff happening at the university. I don't want to go into detail. Juno already had a handgun and she was encouraging me to get one, too. I filled out some kind of form at the police station, and took a quiz, but they said it would be five days before I got my permit."

"Well, lucky you," she said. "The law's changed. Just out of curiosity, what did Juno carry?"

I thought a moment. "Some kind of a Glock nine-millimeter. She said it was fairly light, and safe, and it had—I think—sixteen or seventeen rounds."

"Good memory," Vanessa said wryly, and rose to leave. Marco grumbled a little but rolled onto his back, which he only did when he was sound asleep. At the door, she said, "Get a gun—and a gun safe!—or get an alarm system, maybe both. But whatever you do, *be very careful.* I'll let you know what my PIs tell me about the cars."

Stefan was already in the kitchen washing out the espresso cups and stacking them with their saucers in the dish drain. Just as I was about to press him on what he'd been hiding when Vanessa asked if there was anything we hadn't told her, he said almost absentmindedly, "You still have those gun catalogues, don't you?"

"I'd have to look for them. But are you serious, you really think we should have a gun?"

He turned to me, and shook his head, looking both angry and despairing. "No, I just wondered. After raiding our house, you think the Michiganapolis police would give either of us a gun permit? That's nuts."

There was some wine left, and I poured it out into a new glass, slugged some down the way you're supposed to drink Beaujolais Nouveau, not a fine wine, but I didn't care. I remembered enough about applying for a gun to say, "We don't have criminal records, so there's no reason for them to turn either of us down."

"I don't trust the cops, they'll come up with something. If you or I went in now and applied for a permit, you don't think that'll look suspicious? They'd assume we were planning something, that we were dangerous. I'll call tomorrow about estimates for an alarm system, but that's all we can do."

"Well, that's not all *I* can do. I think I *will* go get a permit."

"They'll never issue you one." I don't know if he was envious or hurt or what, but he was sounding more and more furious, and I did not want to get into a pointless argument. There was no way of knowing if either of us could get a gun permit, but I was sure as hell going to try.

I stayed up late reading online about Michigan's gun laws and I dug out all the catalogues I'd gotten years ago and filed away, thinking I'd never need them. Ruger, Smith & Wesson, Browning, Beretta, Walther. The colored brochures were as thick and glossy and seductive as anything you'd ever seen for a new car. There were also photocopied sheets and tri-fold brochures with listings of local gunnery ranges and The Ten Commandments of Gun Safety.

Tuesday morning, while Stefan was at the gym, I headed to the gun shop whose elderly owner years ago had treated me like a grandson coming to afternoon tea.

The shop was called Aux Armes, in a wry tribute to the French national anthem, I recalled, and looked even more out of place than before in a bland strip mall with a pizza joint and a bank, because several other storefronts were empty, victims of the recession. An old-fashioned bell still hung over the door and jangled as I stepped inside. Tiny Mrs. Fennebresque, a former nurse who'd opened the store as a second career, hadn't changed. She was still dressed in conservative pastels and her cheerful "Good Morning!" was energetic and sweet. She presided over her lovely little shop as if it were a Hummel collection. "Wait—don't tell me—I know you've been here before . . ."

I looked around while she tried to remember. The low-ceilinged space still looked like a cross between a Hallmark store and a hardware store. The shelves were packed with ammunition and cans and boxes, but decorated with silk tulips and hydrangeas in colorful pots. Rifles and shotguns were displayed as reverently as golf clubs along the far wall, with plastic ivy framing them top and bottom. The overhead lighting was bright, but it was softened by pink-shaded lamps in strategic locations, and there were still pots of freesia potpourri scattered about. Clearly the store's appeal was for people like me who wanted a gun, but who also wanted to purge their purchase of anything they might perceive as sordid and lower class.

"I remember now, you're Nick Hoffman," she practically warbled with excitement. "You're the college professor who got in so much trouble. You were a newbie to guns," she added gently, fingering the large fake pearls at her neck.

She wasn't kidding. Back then she'd had to explain the difference between a revolver and a semi-automatic to me, explained safeties, the cost of ammo, everything, until I felt dizzied by all the details about calibers and stopping power and gun weight and recoil and raking and Michigan's gun laws. I'd felt almost paralyzed to be in a gun shop at all, and everything had seemed even stranger because her voice was so sweet, her hair so white, her manner so gentle.

"We talked about a .357 Magnum versus a .22."

"Yes we did!" She was thrilled. "And you brought a very colorful friend back one time. She was a Glock fan, I seem to recall. I saw you one more time after that, and you were not in a good state."

"Yes, someone attacked me on campus."

"Poor boy. I can tell it still upsets you all these years later." She shook her finger at me. "Teddy Roosevelt said that history taught us that the one certain way to invite disaster is to be unarmed. If people knew you had a gun, they would leave you alone," she said.

"That's why I'm here."

"Lovely! I just brewed some jasmine tea, would you like to join me?"

Once again I was drinking tea with her in ivory-colored cups with tiny shamrocks across them, but I couldn't remember the name of the china pattern.

"Belleek," she said, leaning companionably on the counter as we drank tea and I gazed down into her velvet-lined display case where everything today looked inviting. My eyes kept getting drawn back to a Glock 19. It looked simple, clean, deadly. Even the name felt powerful to me.

"Lovely gun," she said. "Reliable, safe, fast. And of course, it's a law enforcement favorite."

I nodded, hypnotized by the way it gleamed under the counter.

"That's the new Gen 4," she said proudly, as if she had designed the Glock herself. "The frame has a rough texture that makes for a better grip." She went on to extoll other features like the dual recoil spring assembly (whatever that meant), but all I could hear was the name "Glock," and all I could think was, "Juno has one, the cops use them, I want one." It was that simple, and that primitive.

"How much?"

"Six hundred."

"Fine, I'll take it."

She smiled softly. "But you'll have to get a permit to purchase the gun, remember—and you haven't even held it to see if it feels like the right one for you. I remember that other time, you decided a .22 would be a good place to start."

"And you said I could handle something bigger."

"Did I? I suppose I did. You probably can." She eyed me carefully. "Why not try it—hold it, I mean." She took it out of the case, handed it to me and I pointed it away from us both, surprised at how uncomfortable it felt.

"Wow, it's heavy."

"That can be good, it can help you keep your hands steady."

I handed it back, carefully, even though I knew it wasn't loaded. "You know, maybe I *will* go with a .22—to start." Just as quickly as I'd decided on a Glock, I'd felt repulsed by the idea of arming myself with anything similar to what the police might have.

"Your hands are on the small side for a man your size," she said. "Here," she said, pointing to another pistol in the display case. "This is a lovely gun. It's a Beretta. Not a large gun at all, but effective. It's safe, simple, practical." She took it out, demonstrated the tip-up barrel, extolled the materials the Beretta was made of, then handed it to me, and once I held it, I wondered if I'd found my first gun. It felt right. I didn't tell her that I had always associated the name Beretta with James Bond, even though he switched to a Walther PPK at some point. That might strike her as frivolous. But I liked the association with secrecy, because I wasn't sure that I wanted Stefan to know I had a gun. Perhaps I'd keep it in our safe deposit box at the bank, or get my own separate box . . .

"People will tell you that a .22 doesn't have much stopping power," she observed. "But if you know what you're doing and can cluster your shots—" She shrugged.

"I'm not planning on shooting anyone," I said.

"Most people don't. But you never know what might happen even when your life is squeaky clean." She gave me a penetrating glance and for a moment I had the strangest feeling that she somehow knew about the police raiding our house.

"That's absolutely right."

She nodded. "You're different," she said. "You've changed. I remember that look from my patients when I was a nurse."

"What look?"

"Somebody who's been through hell. But you don't worry me. I'm not afraid of selling you a gun. Any gun. Nurses get to be psychologists, too, in a way. You may have suffered, but you're not a danger to anyone. You've been through hell, but you've come back."

"That's good to know."

"Don't be fresh! Tell me what happened to that woman who came in with you that time."

"Juno's my boss now."

"Ah, well . . . I seem to recall you live north of campus?"

I nodded and she beamed. "You made quite an impression on me, young man! See how much I remember about you? Well, given where you live, you'll have to go to the North Precinct to start the process of getting a gun permit, and hopefully they won't try to slow things down. They know you professors can be touchy." She chuckled, and I said nothing about Stefan's fears that the local police would never allow either one of us to get a gun permit.

"I would definitely recommend taking instruction at the gun range. It's connected to the university and there's a student and faculty discount. Midweek tends to be a slow time for them, generally." Mrs. Fennebresque handed me a flyer and I thanked her, wished her a nice day, and drove the ten minutes to the precinct building, feeling with each moment I got closer that they would jail me on some phony charge as soon as I walked through the door. "Be calm," I ordered myself. It didn't work. I kept driving anyway.

The northern precinct of the Michiganapolis Police Department was like a small private college. Five low redwood buildings with deep overhangs faced each other around a circle of grass with a huge American flag flying at its center, all of this nestled in the middle of several acres of lawn studded with evergreens and lined with rose bushes. Paths of glazed red brick connected the buildings, and the whole setup reeked of pre-recession spending. And for a public place, it looked awfully secretive and private.

One sign pointed to the fire department, another to service, whatever that meant, and the next to the police. I followed that one to a small public parking lot surrounded by an ornamental four-foot black cast iron fence. The lot was uncrowded and I parked right by a walkway. Getting out of the car I felt grossly conspicuous and wondered if surveillance cameras were monitoring me. And if they were, was the building already on some kind of alert? Wouldn't they assume I was a threat, even though the raid had not panned out? And was this where the SWAT team was based, or did they have their own HQ?

It was hot, and I forced myself to slow down as I walked from my car. I felt lost in some Kafkaesque living nightmare, about to be accused of crimes I hadn't committed but couldn't defend myself against. I remembered every damning and disparaging thing Vanessa had said about the Michiganapolis police. These were not people I could trust, but how else could I get a gun and make myself feel safe?

The entrance was framed in more of those glazed bricks and when I walked into the lobby, I was surprised to see how small it was, and how few chairs were lined against a wall. Maybe they'd changed things since 9/11. "Security," I thought. The smaller the lobby, the fewer people could congregate there and cause trouble, the easier it was to defend the building.

I had remembered it as bigger and less bland, less like a linoleum store. But I'd been there once before to apply for a permit, the last time I'd gone to the gun shop, and backed off after I'd gotten it. Would that count against me somehow? Did they keep records of indecisive people?

"What are you here for?" A portly, sour-faced cop in his fifties was studying me with his blank brown eyes from behind the long security window opposite the door. We were separated by what I assumed was bullet-proof glass, and plenty of steel.

"I want to register a gun. I mean, get a *permit* for a gun. I don't have a gun. I mean, I don't own one, not yet. That's where you come in," I added inanely, and there was a sigh from the cop that clearly expressed not just disgust with local citizens but all humanity.

"Driver's license?"

I managed to get out my wallet and license without dropping either one, and I slid the license through a small security grill opening in the glass window. My hands were sweaty and I could feel sweat dotting my hairline despite the air conditioning. The cop checked the license as carefully as if I were crossing a border during World War II and he was on the lookout for traitors or spies. Then he studied my face.

"Is this your permanent address?"

I nodded, and he handed me a pamphlet to read, slipping through a door behind him with my license. At that moment I started to panic, thinking they'd never give it back to me, that I was trapped, but rather than sit down and even look at the pamphlet, I waited at the window, and he was back sooner than I expected, slipping the license back to me. He nodded at the wall and I went to sit on one of the hard plastic chairs with a hole low in the back uncomfortably close to the butt. They were all like that. Imagine designing something that awful, or buying it.

The grim lobby was well-covered by visible surveillance cameras and I tried not to look at them or anything, anywhere. Then I thought it would seem suspicious if I kept my head down because that's what criminals do to avoid their faces being seen. But how else was I supposed to read what I saw was an official publication about gun safety, just like the one I'd re-read last night at home, and that lay in stacks at Mrs. Fennebresque's gun shop? I skimmed the contents, reminding myself about gun safety in crowds and alone, gun cleaning, storage, and transportation.

The quiet in the lobby was intimidating, and made me almost doubt I was in a police station at all. The cop's phone rang several times, but I couldn't hear anything he said in his cage. I returned the pamphlet when I was done and in return got a quiz on a white sheet of paper. My first time here, I had been surprised to get the pamphlet on loan, so to speak, and to take the quiz on gun safety so soon after reading it.

Fifteen true or false questions covered the identical material I had just read. Was this really how they checked people's gun safety knowledge? It seemed too easy, more like a test of short-term memory, but then as I read the questions, I found the phrasing so convoluted that each one felt like a trap. When I was in junior high school, I'd often had test anxiety, my mind going blank during algebra and other subjects aside from English, and I could feel that incipient blankness and panic returning. I closed my eyes, breathed deeply a few times, and started over. This was not junior high, this was not one of those anxiety dreams where you wake up late and unprepared for something crucial like an interview or a theater performance. I knew I could take the test over another day if I failed this one.

Finished, I brought it up to the counter gingerly and the cop checked the answers right then on his laptop screen. "You got 'em all right." He sounded disappointed. "Okay, now you get some different questions. These are required by law."

I nodded, trying not to appear nervous.

"Do you have any criminal convictions?"

"No, sir!"

He peered at me as if suspecting mockery, but then made a mark on some form. "Are you the subject of any restraining orders?"

"No."

"Okay, that's it, call here this time tomorrow. We issue you the permit, you can buy your gun, and then you register it here. You'll have ten days, then the purchase permit expires." He added as an unconvincing afterthought, "Have a nice day." It sounded more like "Scram!"

15

So what was I supposed to do now that I had crossed a serious boundary in my life I'd never expected to cross? I went to the gym. I didn't need to stop at home first because I always kept an extra set of workout clothes in a small gym bag in the car just in case.

Michigan Muscle was heaven or hell depending on your perspective. Veterans loved it, newbies were overwhelmed and sometimes panicked. It was just so damned big. Over the years it had expanded to over half a million square feet in a weird boxy mix of brick, steel, glass, and concrete. It had no real style, either inside or outside, but it reeked of money spent on the latest equipment, luxurious locker rooms, and an extravagantly severe black and chrome pro shop with matching restaurant.

It was surrounded by parking lots like a mall, indifferently landscaped, and inside, the club revealed itself in stages on many different levels because the site was so sloped and uneven. Pools led to racquetball courts which led to locker rooms which led to offices which led to walkways which led to yoga and Pilates studios which led to cardio rooms which led to stationary biking rooms, all of it seeming to radiate out from the several enormous areas with free weights and up-to-date weight machines. You were always walking up or down or circling back somewhere, and Michigan Muscle could feel like an Escher drawing. Even the profusion of signs didn't help because the additions had been so haphazard. Add to that the relentless neon lights, the wilderness of mirrors and glass doors, and you had quite a bizarre package.

Many people started there and quit, opting for smaller local health clubs where they didn't feel so exposed, so much on stage, or so lost. Some even went to private studios. These tended to be people who had begun working out at their doctor's urging after a heart attack or some kind of accident, and initially thought the supermarket abundance of the club was just right, but eventually found that fine-tuning their needs led them elsewhere, away from the hordes that filled the place most mornings and evenings. I liked it because I could run on the indoor track, swim, bike, do whatever felt right for that day.

I wandered down to the locker room I liked best (there were three each for men and women), trying to decide what exactly to do, when I passed Lucky Bitterman leaving that locker room on the way to—I think—one of the free weights areas. He glared poisonously at me but kept going. Was he following me and pretending not to? Had he somehow gotten inside and changed quickly, or had he arrived in workout clothes?

In the locker room, whose walls had recently been painted lime green to cheer people up, according to the management, I felt my heart beating faster. There were three rows of wooden-doored lockers back-to-back, and lockers along the back and sides of the room forming a U. Facing all of that was a lounge area with widescreen TV, coatracks, counters for towels, and two doors leading to the showers and the adjoining sauna, steam room, and whirlpool beyond. It was a companionable enough place when lots of people were there chatting and changing, but eerie in its own way when almost empty. Noises seemed magnified, so you could be easily startled by a sneaker falling onto a bench, or somebody's belt rattling as he hung his pants inside a locker—and you couldn't be certain where the sound was coming from. Even the silence was ominous. Full-length mirrors studded the locker rooms, and sometimes someone you saw in a reflection was much farther away than he looked—or much closer. Thefts happened now and then, but to my knowledge nobody had ever been mugged in any of the locker rooms at the club. Still, it wouldn't be hard to do. And of course there was the dead body I'd discovered in the sauna years ago, so even worse was possible.

Would Lucky double back and sneak up on me from behind one of the ranks of gleaming wooden lockers?

There weren't many people around anywhere in the gym today. I had decided on weights, because I had this terrible paranoid image of Lucky trying to drown me in the pool, or at least hurt me there.

I didn't see him anywhere, and nodded to the few regulars and trainers I did run into while I worked shoulders and arms, breathing deeply, concentrating. I was able to let go so completely that for half an hour I forgot about the SWAT team and everything that had followed afterwards like a ghastly plague of misfortune. But when I was done, and back in the locker room, I thought I saw Lucky in a towel, reflected in a mirror, going into the shower area that adjoined the sauna, steam room, and whirlpool. Should I leave and shower at home? That suddenly seemed cowardly. I got undressed, slipped on the Adidas slides I wore in the shower, wrapped a big white towel around my waist, and locked my locker with my combination lock.

The sky-blue tiled shower area had ten curtained stalls, but all of them were empty, and I was relieved. When I finished showering off, I headed for the whirlpool and just as I hung up my towel and eased down into the hot, bubbling water, the sauna door banged open and Lucky stomped over. In his towel, he reminded me of Sean Connery in one of the early James Bond films: hairy, fit, devilishly handsome, and dangerous. I may have been able to subdue Stone in Ludington, but Lucky could easily take me down and nobody would know. He was big enough and powerful enough to hold me under the water till I stopped trying to escape. The thought paralyzed me, but even if I wasn't unable to move, I was sitting opposite the metal-railed stair out of the whirlpool, so there was no chance I could have gotten away from him. You just can't make a speedy exit from a whirlpool with the water dragging at your legs.

The showers formed the long part of a capital L and the sauna, steam room, and whirlpool were around the corner in the short part, with the whirlpool all the way at the end. It was too private, too secluded. My breath stopped for a moment as he dropped his towel and stomped down into the water, stood dead center in the whirlpool, the water flowing around the top of his red Speedo, which stretched across his flat, veined belly.

After a moment, he said, "Why the hell are you following me? You drove by my house twice and I never see you in the gym this time of day and suddenly you show up?"

"I'm a member. I'm here all different times."

"And driving by my house? Don't tell me you're thinking of moving and wanted to check out the neighborhood."

"I'm not following you."

Something about the way I said it gave me away; his sour face brightened and he started to laugh. "Wait a minute. You think *I'm* following *you*, right? Oh my God, that is too funny."

I had never seen him smile like this before, or smile at all except contemptuously. He sat down in the water beside me as cheerful as if he were going to give me a hug or at least slap my back like I'd told him the best joke he'd heard in years. Hell, maybe I had. I tried not to recoil and show how he had creeped me out. Up close, the resemblance to Sean Connery was even stronger, and I wondered, trivially, if he had any Scotch ancestry.

"So, why would I stalk you?" he asked companionably. "Because I'm a serial killer who targets bibliographers? Because I hate gay people? Oh, don't tell me, because I'm a general asshole."

I may have turned red.

He was enjoying himself, crossed his arms like a school teacher catching a pupil in an obvious lie. "What, you think I don't know that? I've always been like this, always been a loner. I was an only child, I always got my way, my parents let me flatten them." He shrugged his muscular shoulders. "And now, my career sucks, I'm stuck in Michigan, and I have lymphoma."

I gaped at him. "You look fine, you don't look sick at all."

"On the outside, maybe. My father died of it, so did my uncle."

"But you're young . . ." Between the heat of the whirlpool, the fatigue of my workout, and my impending gun purchase, I felt overwhelmed, which made me even less prepared to sort out Lucky's admissions. Was he bullshitting me? He *seemed* authentic.

"They died younger than I am now. I've outlived them both by three years."

I had not ever expected to feel sorry for Lucky, who had until now been so dismissive of me and Stefan, but I couldn't help being moved now. He apparently saw that on my face and shook his head.

"I don't like you, I don't like Stefan, I don't like anybody much. And I'm not likeable myself. That's just the way it is. And having cancer isn't going to turn me into a sweetheart."

Lucky's gruff honesty was completely disarming. And what made it all the more believable was that he moved away now, sat in front of another set of jets, smiled crookedly, leaned his head back and clearly was ending the conversation. He didn't want sympathy, and he wasn't really apologizing. And yet—

I waited till he left a few minutes later and I stayed in the whirlpool for a while by myself. I did *not* want to walk out of there with him behind me anywhere. I couldn't be sure I trusted him. Hell, I didn't know if I trusted anybody now because someone was still out to get me. Despite what Lucky had said, it could be him and it wouldn't take much to grab me and throw me back down into the whirlpool and crack my skull open on the unyielding tile steps.

I showered off and dried myself, keeping my eyes open and staying alert the whole time, feeling very vulnerable without clothes on, and on slippery surfaces. I hurried back to my locker and got dressed more speedily than usual, and almost shouted when a quiet voice behind me said, "Your towel?" I whirled around and it was one of the black-clad minions who scuttled through the club cleaning up. I thrust my towel at him, he nodded thanks and bore it off to his black laundry cart which I had not even noticed was nearby.

Talk about creepy. Someone more suspicious than I am might have assumed these staffers were all illegal aliens, the way they walked with their heads down and their cap visors shading their faces. They were all short and skinny and anonymous-looking. These worker bees clearly had instructions to not just be as quiet as possible, but noiseless, too, and not to interact with club members in any significant way. If you said "Hello" or "Good Morning" or "Thanks" to one of them, they just nodded and hurried away as if you might be contagious—or the contact could get them fired. I think their self-effacement was meant to increase members' comfort at the club, or sense of privilege, but it annoyed me most of the time, and today, it seemed threatening.

Out in the parking lot, every black car I saw seemed menacing, and my mind filled with visions of carjackings from news stories and movies. If Lucky really was our stalker, the cunning thing to do would be to make a fake confession, then attack me in the parking lot when I was still pondering his pathetic story. The lot was filling up, since it was lunchtime. I had to dodge lots of drivers to get to my car, and even that ordinary action made me picture myself being run over.

Driving home in Michiganapolis's version of lunchtime rush hour traffic, I was sure I was being followed at a distance, but I was also sure I was paranoid and might not be able to trust my perceptions for a long time. It was like what my cousin Sharon told me about what happened to her after brain surgery. The combination of anesthesia still in her body and the morphine for her pain had given her twenty-four hours of hallucinations that were so intense, for weeks afterwards she wasn't sure what was real or not real, whether she'd actually had a conversation or not. "The worst thing is when you stop trusting yourself," she had explained. "And you wonder if you're crazy."

If I told Sharon I was planning to get a gun, I was sure that "crazy" would be one of the first things she'd call it.

Wild ideas went through my head, like stopping at the next light, jumping out and running down the street behind me to see if that particular black car was the Caddy I'd thought I'd spotted before. Or pulling sharply into a driveway, any driveway, and letting that car go by to see if I could spot the license plate or the driver inside. But I went straight home, exhausted by gun shopping, my workout, and my own fear. It was bad enough to feel haunted in bed, unable to sleep because I was reliving the night Stefan and I had been humiliated, or be assaulted by those visions during the day. But I had something worse undermining my stability: I was afraid of myself now, of losing control, of seeing things that weren't there, or imagining the worst.

I found Stefan out on the patio, a bottle of eighteen-year-old Macallan on the table next to his chair. It had been unopened before the night Stefan was driven off to jail. Now it was half-empty, and I hadn't had any. This was the first time I'd seen Stefan with it. Marco was lying on his side on the grass, and he looked up at me sleepily, wagged his tail, and went back to his nap.

"I walked him and fed him," Stefan said, voice slurred, barely turning around to look at me.

"Did you have lunch?" I asked.

"Not hungry."

I wasn't either, though I knew I should be eating after a workout, and drinking water, too. There was another Galway crystal scotch glass on the table, waiting for me. I sat down in the chair on the other side of the low round table, poured myself a few fingers of scotch and drank. It had a good, smooth, oaky burn. Stefan never drank this early in the day, unless we were having brunch. Neither did I. But the raid had unmoored us in so many different ways, that breaking from our habits like this seemed inconsequential.

"I was at the gym," I said, enjoying the midday quiet in our yard and in our neighborhood, though a distant ambulance siren briefly made my jaw clench.

"Yeah, I figured."

"And before that, the police station. To get a gun purchase permit."

"That is pretty fucked up," he said, sipping some more from his glass, and sounding like one of my students. "No matter what Vanessa said, you shouldn't have a gun. I called a couple of security firms about an alarm system, and we could have people out to do estimates any time we want next week."

"Great. Fine. That's not going to stop me from getting a gun."

He sat up, plunked his glass down on the table where it clattered on the glass top, and glared at me. "And what's the point?"

"To defend myself."

"If you'd had a gun when the police came, what difference would that have made?"

"I don't feel safe anymore, you know that."

I couldn't understand why he was so resistant and negative, so determined to argue me out of what I was sure I needed to do. Then I thought about the best defense being a good offense and wondered if he was blowing smoke.

"Why did you lie to Vanessa about not having anything to hide?"

He turned away sullenly, took up his glass and downed what was in it, held the glass against one cheek as if it were an ice pack and he'd been hit and his face was swollen.

"You're lying now," I observed.

He changed the subject: "You've always said America was gun-crazy, and now you've gone crazy, too? How is that possible? I know I said I wished I had a gun, but I wasn't thinking straight, I was humiliated and I wanted revenge. If I can try to get past that, so can you."

You don't need drama and shouting for an argument. A few sharp accusations and questions are enough. We glared at each other, and I understood now what Vanessa had said about incidents like the police raid driving people apart. I wanted to say something even nastier right then. I wanted to hurt Stefan almost as badly as I had wanted to hurt Stone in Ludington, but not physically this time.

"How am I supposed to live with a gun nut?" he said in a low voice.

"How do you live with a gun nut? The same way I live with a Catholic. You'll get over it."

"Fuck you," he said, and stormed back into the house.

"Very mature!" I called, aware that my own comment wasn't much better.

16

They say you should never go to bed angry when you're in a relationship, but we did anyway that night. I took some Benadryl which knocked me out in minutes.

Wednesday morning I found Stefan in the kitchen pulling open drawers and cabinets, banging plates and cutlery, generally making as much noise as he could without actually breaking anything while he put together a sandwich. Marco watched him, hopeful.

He angrily sliced some fresh rye bread, but I didn't say a thing about his sawing away with that big knife and possibly cutting himself. "There are over three hundred million guns in this country that private citizens own," he said, slapping the bread onto a plate. "Three hundred million. Why do you need to have one?"

"How is that a reason for me not to have a gun?"

"You've been proud that you don't fit in, in lots of ways, and now you're one of the sheep."

"You converted, so how are you any different?"

He slammed down the knife, grabbed a smaller one, slathered Grey Poupon onto both sides of the bread, and slapped thin-sliced roast beef on both pieces. It looked messy but good. I registered that, even though our continuing argument had purged me of hunger.

I went after him because he hadn't responded, even though I knew I was wrong to do it. "You're a Christian now—"

"A Roman Catholic."

"Last I heard, they were still Christians. You changed religions. You used to be a minority, now you're in the majority. Fine. It's what you want. It makes you happy. I'm getting a gun. That's what *I* want. What's the fucking difference?"

He shook his head disdainfully, and I despised him at that moment, even as I wondered how it was possible to be so angry at someone you loved and lived with. "Don't compare faith to a firearm—that's just stupid."

"How about trying to sound like an adult when you trash me?"

Stefan bit into his sandwich, staring off behind me, as if willing me to disappear. Then he looked me in the eyes. "You're right," he said, his voice softening.

"What?"

"You're right. I'm *not* being adult. I made a huge change in my life, and you accepted it. Now, when *you're* making a huge change in your life, what do I do? I start freaking out. That's wrong."

Nonplussed, I didn't know what to say. Was he sincere, or was this some kind of reverse psychology?

Stefan took a deep breath. "But it's not the gun, not really. It's that everything seems harder since . . . since what happened, it seems out of whack. I don't even know how I can go back to teaching when fall semester starts, or write anything again. My life doesn't make sense. If I've been touchy about *Fieldwork*, that's why."

"I feel the same way. And then the stalking, the threats, the—" I pointed up in the general direction of the bedroom, not wanting to even say what we had found there polluting our bed.

"Listen, Nick, you want to get a gun? As long as you learn how to use it, and you buy a gun safe to keep it in, that's all that counts." He tried to smile. "At least we don't have kids to worry about. There's no chance Marco could ever get a hold of it without us knowing."

I could feel the fog of hostility inside me clearing. "Thanks."

Marco had wisely kept his distance during our low-key rumble, and wherever he was, he suddenly went barking to the front door. We both froze. And then looked at each other in complete connection and forgiveness, because no matter what the current tussle had been about, we were in this together. It reminded me of one of my favorite novels, *Brideshead Revisited*, where Oxford students Charles and Sebastian feel themselves *contra mundum*: together against the world. It had truly felt all week that the world was leagued against us.

Stefan said, "I'm sorry," as I headed to the door and I called back to him, "Me, too."

Vanessa was there, and I could feel my shoulders relax. "Gotta minute? I left something at home, so I figured I'd stop here on the way back to my office." She looked stunning in some kind of stretchy aqua sheath, with patent leather beige heels and matching shoulder bag. Seeing her was a shot of adrenaline—she was so bright and beautiful and tough. I may have been living in Michigan for a long time, may have considered it my home now, but I still loved New York flash.

She followed me to the kitchen, Marco dancing around her feet as she went. "Hey, kiddo," she said, not ignoring him, but very focused.

Stefan said "Hi" and leaned back against the counter as if bracing himself for bad news.

"Okay guys, your friend in Ludington, he rented his car at Detroit Metro, drove straight to Ludington, didn't leave when stuff was happening to you here in town."

"How can you know that for sure?"

"My PIs are the best, I told you." She winked.

"What about Lucky?"

"Jackpot, maybe. He does drive that model of Cadillac, it's a 2011."

"Sonofabitch!" I said. "He just made me feel sorry for him, I was sure he was for real. He played me!" I told her about our meeting at the gym, and his confession about his illness and his personality.

"Never trust a guy in a hot tub," she said, smiling.

"So is he our stalker?"

"You tell me." She handed me a Post-it. "This is his license plate number. You *have* to get the one on whatever car is following you, the next time it happens. Nobody can do that for you, really. If it matches, well, then it's obvious. Oh, and that dean of yours? He drives an Audi, his wife has a Stingray, so he might be off your list. But my PIs will keep digging. There's nothing they can't find." She grinned a bit mysteriously and made her exit, sleek and dynamic. Juries would either be blown away by her, I thought, or resent her blazing confidence.

Stefan came over to hug me, and we were silent for a moment. "Are you hungry?"

I was, now, and even though I hadn't had breakfast, I was ready for lunch. I broke out some sliced Jarlsberg, half-sour pickles, and the broccoli coleslaw I'd made a few days ago, while he sliced bread for my sandwich. I looked down at the container.

"You made that coleslaw before last Wednesday night," Stefan observed flatly, as if reading my mind. "That was like a different life, it seems like we were different people."

"We were. It's what Vanessa said. We've had easy lives compared to most people and nothing to do with cops, *ever*, real cops, I mean. The worst experience was speeding tickets, and how bad is that?"

We both sighed. In this moment of calm, with the hostility between us having evaporated, I wanted to ask him again what he was hiding from me and Vanessa, but my better angels held me back. As one of Oscar Wilde's characters said, now was not the time for German skepticism. I'd never exactly understood what the quip meant, but that day, it seemed to fit.

We were both restless with Vanessa's news, and we ate standing at the kitchen island, too jazzed to sit down, processing what she'd said.

"Maybe we both need to try and track our stalker?" Stefan suggested. "Or you could drive around hoping he'll follow you, and I'll be further back."

"You really think we can work out the coordination? And if it's Lucky for sure, he doesn't seem predictable. How do we lure him into following me?"

"You could drive by his house a few times and piss him off."

I suddenly felt deflated. "And then what?" I asked. "What proof do we have that he's done all the other stuff? The phone calls—the roadkill—any of it. We'd have to catch him in the act, somehow."

After a moment, I added, "Listen, you're more analytical than I am, while you figure it out, I'm going to check out the campus gun range." I made sure I had the address and left him the pamphlet, now that it was no longer taboo.

SUM had begun as a small agricultural college in the mid-nineteenth century and if you had nothing to do with crop science or soil science or anything like that, it was easy to forget those origins. That is, until you headed south and the buildings gave way to vast acres of farmland and pasturage that felt as far removed from the built-up core of campus as Tibet was from Chicago.

The gun range was at the every southern edge of campus, isolated amid all those green fields. Apparently immune to irony, the university saw no problem with the Garfield range being on Lincoln Road—unless somebody thought the association with two presidents who'd been shot was perversely amusing. The building was low and gleaming, like some kind of health care pavilion, glittering with glass brick and solar panels. I parked in the near-empty lot and headed inside where the terrazzo-floored lobby was so large it felt like some kind of arena. There were several plush seating areas, racks with brightly colored flyers, a snack bar just like you'd find in a gym, and a small information counter. A scrawny, bored-looking guy with fashionable stubble asked if I needed help, and when I explained I was a faculty member and wanted beginner's instruction, he suggested the afternoon class which was only fifteen minutes from now.

The place thrummed with air conditioning so loudly it felt like an ocean liner pulling out of port. I was glad for the noise, since there wasn't any music playing anywhere and the silence made me uneasy.

I signed a waiver that I only skimmed, and looked around guiltily, the way an alcoholic might wonder about seeing someone he knew when he snuck into a bar. I deposited myself on a sofa and shut my eyes, trying to relax.

"Professor Hoffman!" The guy who came to claim me for his class greeted me as if we were cousins reuniting after years for a family wedding. "Hey! Great to see ya!" He was five-ten, swarthy, with green eyes, movie star lips, and large forearms. "Your class in crime fiction three years ago, remember? I wrote that final paper on *Mystic River*?"

"Right . . ." How many students had I taught since that class? Then his name popped up as if on a flash card: "Seamus, how are you?"

He grinned, slapped my back and led me down a short hallway to a bland classroom like hundreds on campus. I was alone, which might have accounted for his enthusiasm. He started a PowerPoint that took me through the parts of a gun and gun safety, explaining everything with the zeal of a real estate broker pushing a house that had been on the market too long. Now and then he read exactly what was on the screen, which seemed a waste of time, but I wasn't going to fault his pedagogy since I loved hearing about the construction of a pistol, how it operated, how the components fit together.

He kept asking "Any questions?" but I just shook my head, taking in the flood of information until I realized he was starting to look a bit anxious. After all, I'd been his professor, maybe he was suddenly a little self-conscious.

"You're doing great," I said. "Really."

He relaxed and went on with his material. Even though I knew the parts of a pistol from research online, I quietly repeated for myself everything he named: barrel, magazine, slide, sights, grip, strap, etc., and all the steps of loading and unloading a gun.

I didn't exactly follow him when he said some people called the magazine a "clip," and that there was a debate in the gun world about which was correct, but nomenclature didn't seem that important an issue right then. I briefly wondered if it might not be better to do this sort of instruction with a group so that other people could ask questions you didn't even know you had, but it was too late for that. I'd made the plunge, there was no point in rescheduling.

When Seamus was done, he told me it was time to go across the lobby. "The center has a terrific filtration system for the lead in the air, and when we go through the first airlock, you'll see a gray strip that looks like a carpet runner. That's for when you leave, to get any lead particles off your shoes. You don't have to rub, just walk along it normally on the way out. And then there are wipes for your hands, too."

"Airlock?"

He nodded. "Two of them. For noise, and for filtration."

Wearing goggles and noise-blocking headphones, I followed him through those two airlock doors into a gun range which looked like a smaller, less elaborate version of the ones I was used to seeing on TV and in movie thrillers. There weren't any big tough cops or soldiers, and there weren't any separations between the small tables people were sitting at. I was mildly disappointed, and had to remind myself we weren't in New York or Los Angeles.

Once again, I was alone, and we took the far left position. The target in my "lane" wasn't human-shaped as I'd pictured it would be.

"The board of trustees won't allow any other kind of target," Seamus explained.

"It's pretty small," I muttered.

The target was just a sheet of 8½ x 11 inch beige paper with a black circle in its center, and that circle was 2½ inches in diameter, he said. Was I really supposed to be able to hit that thing? It hung on a conveyer belt 4½ meters away — that's what the indicator said on the wall, where there was a set of buttons, he explained to me, for bringing it closer, moving it further away, or reeling it in to change the target.

"We can start wherever you want the target placed," he offered.

"No, this is fine."

Seeing a Ruger .22 on the screen in the classroom was nothing like holding one in my hand, and I was glad that he began by repeating what we'd discussed before, showing me how to load the magazine five cartridges at a time, put it into the magazine well, listen for the click, push down on the slide stop, position the gun in my right hand aiming at the target, curl my right pinky, ring, and middle fingers around the grip, secure those with four fingers of my left hand holding the right steady. I did everything slowly, almost as if I were a second instructor telling myself what to do, or an actor studying his own performance, though the word "magazine" suddenly bugged me. I realized I might have to call it a clip or I'd be thinking of *Time* and *Newsweek* instead of ammunition.

The closer we got to firing the gun, the more I slowed down, making sure my right index finger was positioned along the barrel and both my thumbs parallel to each other and down below the slide, since that would pop out when the gun was empty and I could get injured.

"Last move," he said. "Click down the safety with whichever thumb feels most comfortable."

I chose my right thumb, aimed, and took my first shots. The noise wasn't much, neither was the recoil, but hearing the spent cartridges pop out the right side of the gun and clatter onto the table and floor was certainly weird. I dutifully reversed the steps and ended with putting a yellow plastic flag — the empty chamber indicator — into the Ruger's chamber, and set the gun down on the table.

"Good," he said.

But I was disappointed, because from where I sat, it didn't look like I'd done very well. That was until Seamus pressed the button and the conveyer belt brought the target up to the table and I saw five distinct holes inside the black circle, all of them close to the center and each other.

My instructor whistled. "Nice! Have you ever done this before?"

I shook my head.

"That's a great group, seriously. And for your first time, too. Let's try you with the target further back, okay?"

Five cartridges at a time, we went through ninety-five more of them, and even when the target was twenty meters away, I almost always stayed inside the black circle, though the shots weren't as close together as that first time. But I was still surprised—shouldn't this be harder? And how could I have a skill I didn't even know I had?

"Professor Hoffman, you're an awesome shot!"

17

I should have taken some time to just sit in my car in the gun range's parking lot and try to absorb what had happened that afternoon, but I didn't. I drove away elated. It's not as if I was going into a gun battle or even owned a gun yet, but discovering that I had this unexpected talent made me feel less afraid, much less vulnerable. It was all as mysterious as the line I remembered from Don DeLillo's novel *Players* where someone sees a fog rolling in like "a change in the state of information." Mysterious and wonderful.

But even as I felt myself awash in self-congratulation, I knew a skill like the one I'd just discovered wasn't very valuable in my profession. When you cut someone down in academia, you use sneering footnotes, not bullets.

Driving along, I got distracted by an oldie playing on the radio, some synthesizer-driven song by Gary Numan whose title I didn't remember. I turned up the volume anyway as I sped off from the gun range, feeling years younger. It crossed my mind that maybe I should take a self-defense course, too.

Given the distraction and my high, I found myself driving pretty much by automatic pilot to Parker Hall, since I had started at the southern edge of campus to begin with, and I often cut through campus by Parker to get home. Once I was completely tuned in and realized exactly where I was, I decided to stop and look for that mysterious white panel truck I'd seen parked there before, and then check in with my assistant Celine. The truck was there all right, lurking off by itself, and after I parked where I normally did near the back entrance to Parker, I strode over to get the van's license plate. The truck was a Dodge Ram, shiny and new-looking, and I couldn't see anyone in the front seat. But as soon as I circled around the back to check out the license plate, the engine started up and someone drove that thing away from me as if I had a bomb. The van raced off onto campus, squealing around corners.

The driver had either seen me and put their head down when I walked over, or had been in the back and leapt into the driver's seat before escaping. It didn't matter, though, because I got the plate number: SUM 372. The truck belonged to the university. I got out my phone and texted the info to Vanessa Liberati. Whatever was going on, the university was deeply involved.

Upstairs, the message of the day flashing across the electric sign above the EAR reception desk was "Stay Cool!" Bizarrely, Estella was wearing a hippie-style granny dress and shawl; she was starting to seem like an actress who had been hired to wear outré outfits. She smiled absently at me and went back to texting on her sparkly pink phone.

I turned left and headed around the warren of cubicles, and noticed some heads of faculty, but observed once again that people did not look up to see who was coming off the elevator. It was as if they were ashamed of their new, exposed status in the maze of cubicles and just wanted to be ignored. Fine by me.

Then I saw that my office door was open. Celine stood just inside looking agitated. When she spotted me, she rushed forward, grabbed my hands as if to pull me from a fire, dragged me in and shut the door behind us.

"Nick, I was going to call you! We're in trouble!" Her voice was low but frantic and she paced in front of my desk. "I took a later lunch today and when I got back I made myself some tea—" She pointed to the open door connecting our offices and I saw the big purple mug next to her computer.

"I had the creepy feeling somebody had been here. And, well, I *knew* somebody had been here because I could smell the same cologne my husband wears, and it sure wasn't him."

I breathed in deeply and thought I could detect something different in the air. But with my typical Michigan congestion, I wasn't sure what it was, exactly.

"Paul Sebastian," she said parenthetically. "The kids give it to my husband every Christmas."

"You locked the door when you left for lunch?"

"Of course. I always lock it. So I just took a look around in my office and yours, and I don't know, I got more and more paranoid with everything that's been happening to you and to Stefan. When I didn't find anything missing, it seemed worse. Then I thought, what if nothing was stolen, but *something* was left here, you know like—" She grimaced, and I didn't need her to mention the roadkill in my bed.

"Well, I started opening drawers, the file cabinets, and I *still* felt something was wrong, and you know I watch a lot of cop shows, and I just had a hunch that you were being set up, that something bad was planted here. And then I found *this*!" She drew a squarish glassine envelope from the pocket of her purple jeans. Inside was a white powder, what looked like several tablespoons of it.

She set it on my desk and it lay there like some horrible portent in a Greek myth.

"It's not anthrax," I said, surprised at my own calm. "People send that through the mail. In business envelopes." Was I trying to convince myself?

She nodded. "It's probably coke—"

"—or heroin," I said, starting to feel dizzy, plunged once again into unreality. I couldn't believe I was saying these words at all, and in my office, which was about as tame and ordinary a room as possible. It had a desk and chairs and table and book shelves and pictures on the wall just like millions of offices around the country.

"Where did you find it?" I asked, the words coming out with difficulty as I felt my throat constricting.

She blinked her eyes quickly as if trying to shake the image of what she'd seen. "It was taped to the back of your diploma."

We both turned to where my doctoral degree from Columbia hung behind my desk, next to photos of me and Stefan and Marco. It looked blameless enough.

"Someone wants to get you arrested," Celine said. "And fired."

That's when we heard the sirens.

I stepped quickly to the window and saw three campus police cars pull up downstairs in front of the building, roof lights flashing, and the few people nearby stopped as if watching a train wreck. The flashing red and blue was an obscenity on that pretty day in the heart of our bucolic campus.

I backed away from the view, feeling as seared as a vampire exposed to sunlight.

I whirled around. Celine was always so calm and steady, and now her eyes were wide and I could swear her shoulders were trembling. Seeing how terrified Celine was made me feel even more afraid. It was happening again. Me. Police. A raid.

Even inside, with the windows closed and the air conditioning humming, I could hear the car doors slam. Parker Hall with its high ceilings and huge wide hallways was a perfect echo chamber, and within seconds, the sounds of boots pounding inside and up the worn-out stairs was like crazy drums. Why weren't they taking the elevator?

I felt bile in my throat. What had Father Ryan told Stefan? "They're not coming back"? Well, they hadn't come back to the house, but they were *here* at what was my home away from home, and I felt as if I had been crossing a tightrope and slipped, was hanging on with one hand, and any moment I would drop to the merciless floor below where someone had snatched away the net.

Celine shook her head now as fiercely as if she'd been slapped by someone, looked down at the small envelope, grabbed it and rushed into her adjoining office. She opened the envelope and dumped its white powder into her giant tea mug, grabbed a spoon from one of her drawers and stirred it decisively. She left the spoon on a ceramic SUM spoon rest nearby, turned quickly to her shredder, clicked it on and put in the envelope, which splatted through in an instant. She grabbed some other papers and shredded those, too, I guess as camouflage?

"Stay calm," she muttered as we heard what sounded like a herd of policemen heading our way. Before anyone could knock, Celine opened the door with a questioning look on her face, and Detective Valley led half a dozen burly campus cops in. I noted with relief that they weren't dressed for combat, but that flash of relief didn't last as they spread through Celine's office and mine, pawing through books and papers, wrenching drawers open, shoving aside plants and bookends and framed photographs. I could smell the leather of their belts and boots and it sickened me. I felt trapped in one of those recurring nightmares, the kind that wake you up because they're so awful, but have some dark power that drags you back down to sleep again and again.

I forced myself not to look at Celine's tea mug.

"Where's your warrant? You can't do this." I stepped forward when what I really wanted to do was shrink back against the wall closest to my desk.

"We don't need one," Valley said flatly, triumphantly. "You're on university property and campus police can search anywhere we want to for drugs."

I assumed he was correct, and I felt miserably trapped, even without being thrown to the ground and handcuffed. I had no rights here, at least no right to privacy. How was that possible? Had it always been the case? Or had the university's board of trustees quietly changed the ordinances that were supposed to protect the university and everyone attending it? Then I thought about JSOC. I bet he was on it.

"Drugs?" I made myself ask, realizing I'd waited too long to say it. "Are you for real?" I hoped I sounded appropriately outraged and disbelieving, but I doubted it.

I glanced at Celine, who was standing there with her arms crossed. Her eyes were down and she was either ashamed or as freaked out as I was, and found watching the uproar in our offices unbearable. The energy in those two rooms was more than negative, it was poisonous verging on destructive, barely restrained. The cops didn't just want to find what had obviously been planted, they would have enjoyed hurting us, or me, anyway. I felt their coiled anger, their dormant violence, and it was beyond intimidating each time they passed one of us. They might have had their own force fields that had the power to consume us, and the offices seemed to get smaller and smaller each minute.

Time seemed to crawl and the cops were as unreal and inimical to me as the Black Riders in *The Lord of the Rings*. I remembered what Vanessa had said about how lucky we'd been not to have our house trashed, but if the cops stayed here much longer, they would start breaking things in their frustration, I was sure of that. Because unless they'd planted more than one envelope, they weren't going to find anything, even with all their pawing the underside of desk drawers and peering behind file cabinets which they yanked away from the walls.

Like Celine, I couldn't even look at them. Except for Valley, standing there turning around slowly like a lighthouse beacon, they were a blur of blue uniforms. I fought the desire to shout or to retreat entirely into myself and pretend this wasn't happening. I made myself remember the physical sensations of being at the gun range just a little while ago, filling my mind with the sound and feel of firing the Ruger again and again. The deeper I went into that mental scene, the stronger I felt. I was a good shot. I wasn't powerless. I wasn't a victim.

So I challenged Valley: "Who told you there were drugs here?"

He snorted derisively. "We don't reveal who our informants are."

"Maybe you don't have one. Maybe you just enjoy harassing people. How do I know you're not full of shit?"

His eyes narrowed and he stepped closer as if he wanted to punch me, and that's when I could smell his cologne. Celine was just a few feet away. I glanced at her and she looked up, shrugged quickly and shook her head. I don't know if Valley saw this byplay, but he barked out an order: "Check *all* the pictures."

The team of cops pulled every print and photo off the walls, and I'm sure I heard some glass crack as they turned every single one of them around. All of the cops called out "Clear" one-by-one as if they were paratroopers storming some suspected terrorist den. Vanessa wasn't kidding. They were just police, campus police at that, but they thought they were soldiers on the front line.

Valley was grim, stomping around now and glaring at the papered backs of the frames that the cops were leaving stacked haphazardly on the floor, against the windows, anywhere.

"Out!" Valley shouted when it was clear they weren't going to find what he obviously expected they would.

Juno Dromgoole appeared at the door, looking severe and matronly in a gray and black houndstooth suit and black pumps. Valley shoved past her and I could have sworn he hissed, "Nothing!"

She stepped into my office as if it were toxic somehow and glanced around with loathing. "Look what you've done," she said with withering contempt.

"Bullshit. The campus police did this."

"You need to seriously think about a leave of absence—"

"No. *You* need to think about defending faculty from storm troopers." I didn't like playing the Nazi card, since America was awash in that kind of hyperbole, but right then I would have given her a derisive "*Zieg Heil!*" myself if she hadn't turned and left.

But I wasn't finished. I said, "What will you do when they start throwing black hoods over our heads and dragging us off for interrogation in some basement somewhere? Wave goodbye?"

I slammed the door after her, hoping that it made her jump. I had no idea exactly who else was out there on the department floor aside from funky Estella, and I didn't care.

Celine was chuckling. "I've never heard you yell at anybody," she said.

"Juno deserves it. She's become a fascist."

Celine shrugged. "They all do, when they're administrators. It's like *The Invasion of the Body Snatchers*. They look the same, but they've been hollowed out and replaced."

I walked over to give her a quick hug. "You were brilliant. I couldn't have thought that fast."

She thanked me.

"Now we have to clean up," I said.

"Yeah. And fumigate."

We shut the doors and got to work. I didn't say it, but if my office did have hidden camera surveillance, somebody would have seen Celine dump the powder and shred the envelope. So we were safe, but only up to a point.

"When you put stuff back, check everything for bugs," I said.

"Already on it," Celine replied.

They'd emptied the desks and rifled the books and it took an hour to put our offices back together. Though I was quietly furious at what the campus police had done, I realized it could have been much worse. The glass on one Seurat print *had* cracked, but having it replaced wouldn't be a big deal. They wanted us to feel scared and violated, and they'd only partially succeeded in their mission. Yes, I did feel like a survivor of an explosion who was disoriented and couldn't hear quite right, but I was still standing, still functioning, and angry as hell, not crushed. We'd thwarted Valley—and apparently Juno—in getting rid of the drugs, if that's what that powder had been. But what if it was something harmless, meant as a warning of some kind?

"They won't try it again," Celine said, falling into her office chair, and sighing. But then she jumped up, grabbed her mug and some

Palmolive dish soap from a desk drawer. "Bathroom," she said. "I have to wash this out."

While she was gone, I opened up the shredder to see if I could find the traces of that envelope. I couldn't detect anything in that chaos of paper strips, but was it safe to leave the stuff there. What if Valley and his minions came back and did an even more thorough search? I stepped out to the reception desk to ask Estella if she'd seen anyone heading to my office.

"A bunch of cops?" she said tentatively. "Oh, and Dr. Dromgoole."

"No, before that."

She winced as helplessly as if I'd asked her to define a subatomic particle. "I don't know," she confessed. "I was, like, texting my boyfriend." She grinned dopily.

"Okay, thanks."

I headed back to my office, wondering if the law considered a man's office as his castle, or was it just his home. And did that even matter since we were on a college campus.

I asked Celine what she thought about the shredder when she came back with her washed-out mug and the dish soap. She wordlessly set them down on her desk, found a brown paper shopping bag in another drawer, emptied the shredder refuse into it, folded it up tightly and put it in her large shoulder bag. She took a can of Lysol from a bottom desk drawer, thoroughly sprayed the inside of the shredder container and dried it with paper towels.

"I *know* they're not going to risk stopping a black woman and searching her without a warrant," she said. "Because I will *work* their last nerve if they mess me around. I will sue their asses for discrimination and the stink will go national."

She was dead right. As oppressive and intrusive as the university had become, it feared bad publicity that could go viral, feared the blizzard of tweets and YouTube videos that would flood the Internet if it made that kind of misstep.

"Was it the same cologne?" I remembered to ask. "Was Valley wearing what you thought you smelled after you got back from lunch?"

"I don't know, Nick. I'm not sure. I was too agitated."

I sat down at my desk, the Herman Miller chair suddenly feeling as comfortable as a soak in a hot tub. Could Valley really have been behind everything that'd hit me and Stefan this past week? Why? He didn't like me, but that was nothing new. He didn't like most faculty, openly considered them nothing more than over-educated miscreants, carriers of the disease of chaos. But why go after me and Stefan *now*? We had not run into each other in years and there was nothing we'd done back then that would have precipitated such a campaign of harassment and revenge. Or was Valley doing someone else's dirty work? The dean? Juno? Both of them? It wasn't paranoid to ask these questions because someone really *was* out to get us, and was hitting harder every time. If drugs had been found in my office, I could have ended up not just fired, but arrested, imprisoned, and likely unable to work anywhere again as a professor. Who'd hire me after being fired from SUM in disgrace, and with a felony conviction on my record?

My face must have betrayed some of this, because Celine grabbed my arm fiercely and said, "Nick, we're going to get the bastard who did this to you. I don't know how, but we will."

18

I left campus in a daze and drove around town, unwilling to go home where I'd have to tell Stefan about this new outrage. He'd been through more than enough trauma already. Reporting the cops and Valley in my office would be like letting go of someone's arm when you'd been dragging him out of quicksand. How could he not sink?

So I drove. But where could I go? Where could I *ever* go to escape what had just happened, what had retriggered the shock of the SWAT team night? Away from the scene, down from whatever ledge I'd climbed onto when I'd shouted at Juno Dromgoole, I thought it impossible that the scars of this week would ever heal. There was no closure possible, only deeper immersion in shame. It didn't matter that we lived in a small city with only one major newspaper and that the paper hadn't reported what had happened at our house. It didn't matter that my name wasn't being bitten into like a breakfast donut by tens of thousands of people, mocked by some, defended by others. The exposure and humiliation I'd already suffered was enough. It was inside now, searing me like a brand.

I ended up heading home with a weird sense of defeat, and was glad that only Marco was home, needing attention, dinner, and a walk. Stefan still wasn't back when I returned from the walk, and I didn't bother calling him. I was glad to be alone with my own thoughts, and I fell asleep in bed watching one of my favorite classic noirs, *Laura*, Marco by my side.

When I woke up Thursday morning, Stefan was snoring, which meant he must have taken one of his sleeping pills since that was the only time he snored. I was grateful, because that meant more time before I had to tell him about Valley and the campus cops descending on my office. So

I showered, got breakfast for me and Marco, walked him, and when I returned, Stefan still hadn't woken up.

I didn't have a therapist, hadn't had one in half a dozen years because my life seemed so placid, but now I thought I needed to talk to someone I could trust. Father Ryan popped into my head for some reason, so I drove to St. Jude's, hoping to find him. I knew he was often there in the mornings before Mass.

Michiganapolis had two downtowns in a way, one centering on the state capitol west of campus, the other around the university, and St. Jude's was on a cul-de-sac near campus, well inside the smaller, less built-up downtown. The short, dead-end street was the typical mélange of moderately priced ethnic restaurants and clothing stores, but St. Jude's was near the end where the commercial buildings gave way to fine old houses and older trees and then a public park. Given the bosky setting, the unadorned vaguely Gothic brick façade and bell tower brought to mind a rural church. I parked across the street, put as many quarters in the meter as I had on me, but before I made it over to the steps, I saw Father Ryan emerging in his "clericals." He looked surprised, then waved, and I dashed across to ask if he had some time for coffee. There was a Starbucks a block and a half away.

"That's where I was going, Nick." He studied my face as we walked over. "Are you okay?"

"Not really. The campus police raided my office yesterday. I haven't even told Stefan yet."

He looked stunned as we walked into Starbucks, which was almost empty. Coffee shops of all kinds had proliferated in town and you never knew when they'd be filled with students on their laptops, or nearly vacant.

I bought us both frozen mocha Frappuccinos and we settled into a corner where nobody could hear us, far from the counter and the baristas, far from the door, and far from the floor-to-ceiling windows. The interior was a small maze of worn leather armchairs and tiny tables, and not my favorite place in town for coffee, but it was close by, and I wanted to sit down with Father Ryan as soon as possible, not wander.

I'd never been alone with Stefan's spiritual guide before, and it struck me as a little odd. In just a few short years, he'd had a profound impact on my partner, though he discounted his influence and said he was just journeying along with Stefan.

Today, his fashion model good looks didn't register on me with the discordance they usually did. His face was like a beacon: clear, open, safe. I could understand why Stefan had been drawn to the door Father Ryan had opened for him, and then stepped through into another faith. He radiated a sense of calm, even though he had clearly been disturbed by what little I'd already told him.

"Tell me what else happened, Nick."

I did, trying not to rush, and after the initial shock, his face settled into grave concern. At one point, he said, "Careful—your hand is shaking."

I put my coffee down and took a few deep breaths.

"At first I thought you wanted to talk to me about Stefan," he said, "ask me something, and I was going to tell you I couldn't share anything he's told me in confession, but you probably know that?"

I nodded.

"Are you sure you don't want to go home? Wouldn't you feel better there? I can drive you if you're feeling unsteady. We'll figure out your car later."

"I'll be okay." Then I contradicted myself: "I feel lost, Father."

"How do you mean?"

"Lost in what's going on with me and Stefan. I mean, what's happening to us. I don't feel like the same person anymore."

He nodded. "You're not. Disaster changes us. It's inevitable."

"But what if it's made me crazy?" I lowered my voice and leaned forward. "I've been to a gun range. I applied for a permit to buy a *gun*."

He grinned. "I'm from northern Michigan. I grew up with guns, I have half a dozen, so that doesn't sound crazy to me at all. If you want to go shooting together sometime, let me know."

"Really?"

"Really."

I went on to explain the most recent blows Stefan and I had experienced leading up to the raid on my office. His face grew even more pained as I went on. And then something unexpected popped out: "You told Stefan they weren't coming back." It sounded like an accusation, and I felt myself blushing.

He sighed. "It wasn't a promise, it was something to hope for, to hold on to. It seemed reasonable at the time."

"You're not going to tell me to turn the other cheek, are you?"

He flashed a neon smile. "No, that would be glib. And probably dangerous."

My thoughts were jumbled and I wondered now why I had even sought him out. Could anyone help me?

He said, "Tell me who you think is tormenting you."

I ran through the short list of suspects with him. He dismissed them all.

"That professor—Lucky?—sounds miserable, but not like he has the energy to launch a campaign like this. And your chair or the dean? That's not how these people operate. I've known enough academic types. If the administration wanted to get rid of you, they'd be more subtle. Bureaucracies may be cumbersome, but they're devious when they need to be. They dread scandal more than disease."

"You're right," I said. "Wait a minute! That scandal line, it's from Edith Wharton."

Ryan nodded. "*The Age of Innocence*. My mother was an English teacher. She adored Wharton. It rubbed off."

"Are you kidding? How come I didn't know that?" I wondered if Stefan hadn't told me more about Ryan because he thought I would suspect him of making it up to curry favor with me, given that I was a Wharton scholar.

"Really, scratch those people off your list," he insisted quietly.

"But bureaucracies are so twisted and power hungry, they eventually become evil, and whoever is after us *has* to be evil," I said. "Stalking us, or me anyway, setting a SWAT team on us, breaking into our house, putting roadkill in our bed, provoking a drug raid . . ."

"Well, Nick, I'm careful about using the word evil. Even Christ forgave on the cross. 'Forgive them Father for they know not what they do.' His killers *did* something evil, but that doesn't mean they *were* evil. I will say this, though: whoever's orchestrating the campaign against you must be suffering inside, suffering profoundly, and is trying to make you suffer just as much. Who do you know who'd feel like that? Anyone?"

If that was the explanation, then I couldn't think of a single person, and my frustration burst out in a totally unexpected way. "Stefan's hiding something from me. He knows something about that guy's suicide and he won't tell me what it is."

"What guy?"

"His student, you know, the one who Stefan caught plagiarizing? His name was Casey. The poor kid freaked out and hung himself in Parker Hall, remember?"

Father Ryan frowned, and I found myself wondering if he knew more about the suicide than he could tell me, whether through Stefan, or some other way. Or was that being overly suspicious? He took a long sip of his coffee drink, then said, "People claim secrets are bad things in a marriage. Sometimes they help keep it going. Sometimes not. You'll have to find out which kind this is."

"How?"

"Ask him, if it's important to you."

"I have, and he pulled away."

"Give him time, then." He added, "Love is patient, love is kind," and I recognized the famous words.

"Corinthians," I said.

He grinned. "Looks like we know each other's favorite writers."

I finished my coffee, and I asked him, "How are you so relaxed about me and Stefan—as a couple, I mean?"

"Well . . . my sister is a lesbian. But even if she wasn't, the Church has got some of its current theology dead wrong. My feeling is, if it ain't love, it ain't God."

"Wow. Do you say that in church?"

"Of course I do. And yes, some people complain to the bishop, but he hasn't slapped my hand yet, so I'm okay."

Before I could ask anything more, I happened to look up. There was nobody blocking my view of the front window, and on this bright spring day I could see a black car double parked across the street. That wasn't common in Michiganapolis, and I stood up to go to the window. I couldn't see the face of the driver, but it was clearly a man at the wheel, and when I opened the door and stepped outside, he sped away at easily twice the speed limit. Much as I hated the police, I hoped he'd get stopped for speeding, hoped he'd crash into something.

But even if nothing stopped him, at least I got the license plate number of the car: DXM 838. When I walked back inside and felt the soft cocoon of cold air, even the bored-looking baristas with hipster black-framed eyeglasses and beards had woken up and were staring at me. So was Father Ryan.

"That was the car!" I said, sitting back down and getting my phone out to text Vanessa Liberati. "It has to be the one that's been following me. And it *wasn't* a Chrysler, it was definitely a Caddy."

"For a minute, I thought you were going to chase him down the street," Father Ryan said softly, and I realized how hard I was breathing, almost as if I had been running. I flashed on the image of that shape-shifting Terminator chasing Linda Hamilton in one of the movies, grim, determined, inescapable. If only I had that kind of power.

"I need to go home. Thanks for your advice."

Ryan calmly thanked me for the coffee and I hoped he didn't think I *was* crazy.

As soon as he saw me walk in, Stefan asked, "What happened?"

While I sat cross-legged on the floor in the living room with Marco nuzzling and mouthing my hands in greeting, I told Stefan the whole horrible story of yesterday's drug raid. I didn't exaggerate, but I didn't leave anything out, and I didn't look up at him once because I was sure meeting his eyes would send me over the edge. With all my recitals of bad news, I was beginning to feel like the Ancient Mariner.

"Omigod," he said when I was done. "Omigod—omigod—omigod." He was sitting on the edge of one of the armchairs opposite the fireplace, head in his hands, rocking back and forth like a mourner at a funeral. "This is never going to stop."

Strangely, instead of being unnerved by his despair, I suddenly felt the opposite. I felt confident, I felt brave.

"It *has* to stop," I said. "We'll find out who's behind everything and we'll *make* it stop."

He mumbled through his hand, "How?"

"Hell if I know," I said, and he looked up, apparently startled by my flippant tone. But what I said amused him and he laughed a little, tentatively, and that grew and grew until he was taken over by laughter like an infant having its belly tickled. Pretty soon he had tears in his eyes and Marco started leaping up at him to participate in the fun.

"I need a drink," I said, even though we hadn't had lunch, and Stefan followed me to the kitchen where I poured us each several fingers of Lagavulin and let Marco out into the backyard. We didn't usually drink smoky single malts in the spring, we preferred lighter scotches, but nothing was normal anymore. I set the kitchen radio to play something soothing by Thomas Tallis and I dug out some smoked salmon spread from the fridge. I toasted salty bagels in the four-slice Breville toaster my cousin Sharon had sent us for Christmas and Hanukah. She had initially taken Stefan's conversion better than I had, coming at it from her perspective as a cancer survivor: "Be thankful he wasn't diagnosed with something life-threatening and that's why he chose a new path. He wasn't desperate or afraid of dying. He felt *called*. You're lucky."

Stefan and I sat at the granite-topped island, drinking and munching companionably. It's not just strangers who can be knit together by sharing a meal; even spouses can deepen their connection, heal a rift, arm themselves against adversity, can do almost anything through the quiet magic of food and drink. Sitting there, I remembered the times the electricity had gone out in our neighborhood because of a thunderstorm and how we'd huddled around LED emergency lanterns, feasted on bottled water, peanut butter and crackers as if they were the offerings of a fine chef, relieved that we were together, that our house was unscathed, that we hadn't lost any trees, that life would go on, order would soon be restored.

I couldn't tell you why, but that's how I felt right then, grateful and even mildly hopeful.

Then the mood changed when I said, "Father Ryan told me we should look for somebody who's suffering the way we are—"

"You talked to Ryan? Why? When?" Stefan looked almost angry.

"We had coffee just now."

"Why?" He set his scotch glass down as if he wanted to smash it but was forcing himself not to.

"Why not? I didn't know who else to talk to and I thought he could help. He did. I can see why you like him. I mean, we didn't talk about religion or anything like that, but he's pretty calm and centered." None of that seemed to be getting through to Stefan, whose face was still beclouded. "Are you pissed I didn't tell you first?"

He flushed. "Yes. Sort of."

I took his arm. "Stefan, I was a wreck yesterday and I was relieved you weren't home. And this morning, you were sound asleep. Did you really think I'd wake you up for something like that? I needed to calm down first, and talking to him really helped." Stefan didn't pull away, which I considered a good sign. "I know you tell Ryan things you don't tell me, and that's okay. He's your priest, you go to confession, I get all that."

"It's called reconciliation now, not confession." Stefan knocked back his scotch and poured another two fingers of it.

"Oh, sorry. I guess he called it confession so I'd know what he meant."

Stefan wasn't really listening. He said, "There's something I haven't even told Ryan, not all of it, anyway. I haven't told anyone."

"It's about that student's suicide, isn't it?"

He nodded, his face as twisted with guilt and shame as if he were a gargoyle carved by a medieval stonemason to represent those cruel and terrible feelings.

19

Since the night last week our lives had been torn apart, my sense of time had been completely disrupted, and while I waited for Stefan to tell me what he'd been hiding, I realized once again how I had been cut adrift from the very ordinary markers I took for granted: regular meals; watching our favorite TV shows; walking and feeding Marco the same time every day, day after day. It's as if I was living in some kind of perpetual, fogged-in present which became murkier no matter what I did or said or thought. Was it any wonder that I was so tired? Deep down, I felt lost.

And things were even worse, because despite brief moments of calm or at least quiet at home, there was still a gulf between me and Stefan, one we had not even looked into, let alone talked about. I would never truly understand the horror he had experienced being dragged off by the cops, those endless poisonous moments that I doubted any amount of therapy or prayer could vanquish. I had lived those moments vicariously in movies and TV shows, but when they were over, the catharsis I felt was secondhand, an artifact of someone else's imagination. Now, there was no relief. His experience was an abyss I couldn't plumb.

And my helplessness and panic, those would be alien to *him*. We had experienced the police assault together, but it wasn't like being in a tornado shelter with the winds howling outside and tearing at the doors, and then finally emerging after the devastation was over. No, he had been swept away and I'd been left behind, and though we were reunited, we would always be separated by the difference of those hours. I would always be the one who had suffered less than he had, the one who had not been so utterly humiliated.

And how much longer would our relationship last with a minefield like that between us? It was as deadly as the death of a child, which many couples never survive. Tragedy didn't always unite couples—often it sundered them forever even if they went through the motions and pretended they could go on together.

"It's my fault that student, Casey, committed suicide," Stefan brought out.

"*What*? What are you talking about? Because you caught him plagiarizing and confronted him? Stefan, you did what was right. And you gave him a second chance, didn't you? To do another paper? That was pretty generous. Most professors would have flunked him for plagiarism."

Stefan waved that away. "Casey didn't hear any of that, not really. He was crying, Nick. He told me that he wanted to kill himself."

I was about to say Casey was just being dramatic, but I didn't even start the sentence. It hadn't been teenage angst, it was real. The boy *had* hanged himself, after all. But why?

Stefan went on as if he'd read my mind. "Casey said his parents were very strict about his grades, they'd home schooled him for years until SUM, and still looked at all of his assignments. He said there was no way he could hide what happened. They'd get it out of him somehow. He didn't know how to keep secrets. They wouldn't let him. They were relentless."

"Sounds like he grew up in a prison. But what were you supposed to do about it? I know therapists have—what's it called?—a duty to warn, if they think a patient is going to hurt someone or hurt themselves, right? But you weren't his shrink. Anyway, how could you have known he was serious?"

"I *did* know," Stefan said blankly.

"What?"

Stefan hugged himself and looked down. "It was in his eyes. He was *terrified*. I've had students try to snow me before. This wasn't fake, this wasn't bullshit. It was *real*." He closed his eyes, shook his head, and I now found myself wishing he would stop.

"And—" Stefan hesitated, then finished his sentence in a rush: "And I just didn't want to get involved." Now he sat back and frowned. "I even lied to the campus police when they spoke to his professors and asked if he could have some reason to kill himself. I said 'Yeah, well, lots of students have problems, who has time to listen to them all?'

They probably thought I was an asshole, but I couldn't risk saying anything."

"Risk how?"

"Come on, he hanged himself in Parker Hall and I was the only one of his profs who had an office there. The cops asked me if he was trying to send me a message. I told you that last year when it happened." Now he looked mildly aggrieved that I wasn't following every twist and turn of his recital.

I didn't remember that part about lying to the cops, but the whole episode had been so freaky I had probably blocked things out to make walking into Parker Hall afterwards more bearable. It was where I had to work. It was where I'd probably be working for the rest of my career. I had no tolerance for ghosts.

"But there wasn't a suicide note, right? I remember there wasn't. That's what I don't understand."

Stefan shrugged. "Maybe there was, and his parents destroyed it."

I shook my head. It didn't add up. It had never added up.

And then I got a text on my phone. It was from Vanessa and read "Car's owner Pat Silver. 4022 Tuberose. I'm in court now. Don't do anything. Let's talk later."

"I have to go," I said, not explaining.

Stefan sighed and said, "Whatever." He didn't ask where I was going or why, proof of how the SWAT team's raid had sundered us and killed his spirit. He hadn't been in jail long, but he had the defeated, shrunken air right then of someone whose spirit has been broken by prolonged incarceration, someone rendered unfit for a world without bars.

Stefan said he might as well go to campus for the afternoon to try to do some work. I didn't need to ask why he couldn't work at home. Our home had become toxic. What were we supposed to do about that? I couldn't even imagine moving.

I headed off to Pat Silver's address in what was called Roseville, a small 1930s-era enclave in Michiganapolis where all the streets had names like Bellerose, Wildrose, and Rosebush. Its small brick or stone houses were like English country cottages more than mid-Michigan homes. You know, diamond-paned windows, curving brick paths, urns filled with annuals or twisted topiaries, the works. Streets in Roseville were lined with oaks, and the gardens were some of the prettiest and best-tended in the city, thanks to an overbearing neighborhood association—or so I'd heard.

I'd never been a thrill seeker, had no interest in rock climbing, bungee jumping, parasailing, or any even partly extreme sports. Hell, I'd never even tried a roller coaster or a helicopter ride, but that past was in shreds. Flushed and breathing hard, I was aware that going to confront this Pat Silver guy was probably nuts, maybe even dangerous, but I didn't care. I wanted to see the man who was stalking me and Stefan and trying to ruin our lives, look him in the eye and demand to know what we had done to make him torment us. I wanted the craziness to end. That was all I could think about, all I could see ahead of me. Resolution. Escape.

The postcard prettiness of Rosedale as I drove along might have soothed me at any other time, but now I imagined throwing bricks through decorative bow windows, smashing wildly ornamental mailboxes, ripping shake shingles off roofs. And I had the strange sense of dispassionately watching myself at the wheel: enraged, exhausted, and unpredictable.

I picked out the large street numbers 4022 and the name "Silver" on a wrought iron mailbox smothered in purple clematis. I parked halfway down the shady street from it. Pat Silver's lair couldn't have been cuter, with white roses climbing up the ochre stucco'd walls and tubs of pink hydrangeas flanking the arched red door. Grandma's house, I guess. What would the Wolf be like?

The street was quiet except for the birds: plaintive mourning doves and chickadees, and arrogant crows.

But before I got out of my car I saw a woman with a blue mesh shopping bag come limping down the far end of the block. She turned in at the same address I had been texted. She must have been Silver's wife. Her middle-aged face under a helmet of white hair was grim, but the rest of her fit in with the neighborhood as if she were an extra hired for a film scene: puffy white peasant blouse, calf-length cream and pink flowered skirt, pink sandals. I waited till she had let herself in, then headed down the block for her door, still feeling I was separated from myself, a spectator, not an actor. I'd been sitting in an air-conditioned car and hitting the street made my forehead damp. I tried wiping it with the back of my hand.

I walked up the red brick path and as I stood before the red door with its door knocker shaped like an angel's wings, I felt insanely reckless and free. I had no way to defend myself from whatever was on the other side of that door, but I was facing it nonetheless. I rang the brass doorbell and the chimes played some song I didn't recognize.

The door opened slowly, and the woman I'd seen entering a few moments before stood there surveying me.

"I want to talk to Pat Silver."

She glared at me. "Took you long enough. Come in, then." She stepped back.

Completely nonplussed, I entered a low-ceilinged living room as picturesque as the whole street: everything was unbearably cute chintz and china figurines of shepherds and shepherdesses. The only decoration on the walls covered in a shiny pink-and-white-striped paper was framed photos of men in U.S. Army uniforms, and enough Celtic crosses to stock a small gift shop.

"I'm making tea. Sit down."

I had entered the Twilight Zone.

I picked an armchair near the door in case I had to make a quick exit. She hadn't locked the door behind me. The chair was stiff and unyielding. From the kitchen I could hear the local classical radio station; at least that's what I assumed it was, since the hosts played Brandenburg concertos several times a day and one of them was playing now. I never could remember its number, only that I intensely disliked the implacable cheerfulness.

If I'd been sweaty before coming in, now I felt my skin as dry as if I'd been walking into a fierce wind. Well, hadn't I?

As the woman limped back into the room with a tea tray, I wondered where to start. And what the hell had she meant by saying it took me long enough?

She eased into a chair near mine with an elaborately carved tea table between us and proceeded to fuss with cups and sugar. Her bad leg jutted out at an ungainly angle, but she seemed used to that. The blue and white tea set with Chinese scenes on it was very pretty and I'd never seen one like it before. She must have caught my inquiring glance.

"Churchill," she explained. "It was my grandmother's."

I thought to myself that Stefan would tell me it was crazy to have tea in our persecutor's house, but though this woman lacked any emotion, I did not feel I was sitting in a nut house, which puzzled me.

She handed me a cup after asking how I liked it, and then before I could take a sip, she said, "Why so long? Somebody should have come long ago to apologize, somebody should have come *last year*."

"Apologize? For what?"

She clanked her cup down in its saucer and some tea spilled over the side. "Are you kidding me? You people at the college are all the same." She was one of those townies who insisted on calling SUM "the college" as if to reduce its size and diminish its importance. "You're so high and mighty. If you're not here to apologize, what *are* you here for?"

I gulped down some tea, confused and wondering if I was even in the right house. "Where's Pat Silver?" I asked. "That's who I want to talk to."

"*I'm* Pat Silver. My parents wanted a boy and they got me instead," she added, with the weary note of having explained her name not being short for "Patricia" thousands of times.

We glared at each other and I felt idiotic holding my tea cup when the atmosphere was electric with tension. I set it down carefully. "Do you own a black Chrysler 300? License plate DXM 838?"

"Yes."

A *woman* was behind all our distress? How was that even possible? Hadn't it been a man threatening me on our street? Unless she was conspiring with someone . . .

"So why have you been persecuting me and my partner Stefan?"

She flushed and said, "Jesus, Mary, and Joseph. I haven't been doing anything to you or to anyone else. I don't even know you. I mean, I know your face from the newspapers, and that you teach English. That's why I thought you were here, to apologize for your colleagues, for the school." She sniffed. "I expected somebody higher up, but I guess I'm not important enough for any of those muckety-mucks."

"Wait a minute. Apologize for what? Someone's been after *us*, stalking us—"

"Is that why you're here? Because you think I've done you wrong? That's crazy! *You're* the one in the wrong, you and all those creeps at the college who turned my poor boy's head. You're all commies and queers!

You killed my son, or as good as did it. Casey was going to be like his brothers and his uncles and both his grandfathers and go into the Army until he started taking those godforsaken English classes and got his head all screwed up. Who cares about books? They're dead, they've always been dead. Why did you all encourage him like that? You poisoned his mind and you turned him against his family, against his tradition. He could have had a real life in the Army, a good life, and now he's dead all because of you."

Casey. *This woman was Casey Silver's mother!* The boy who had hanged himself in Parker Hall last year. And she thought I had come to say I was sorry for his suicide? So that's why she had invited me in, that's why she was going through this bizarre act of serving me tea. Why hadn't I put their two names together as soon as I got the text?

Her face darkened. "You say someone's been, what, following you? Tell me what else."

I told her about the SWAT team, and the two threatening phone calls, being threatened and followed, about when our house was broken into, and the raid on my office (but not about the planted drugs we had disposed). It was an edited version of what Stefan and I had been through over the last week, but it was chilling enough, and with each detail, she shrank back into her chair, ending up looking as appalled as Scrooge seeing Marley's grim chains.

I asked, "Does anyone else have access to your car?"

She nodded warily. "My husband," she murmured. "Even though we're separated and he has his own car, he still keeps a set of keys to mine." The way she said it, I could tell this was not something that made her happy. "He uses the car whenever he wants to, and I don't drive much myself. He also comes and goes here, even if I change the locks." She rubbed her bad leg unconsciously, it seemed.

Watching her hand, I had to ask, "Did your husband do that to you?" And I wondered who the hell he was, and where.

She snapped at me. "No. *I fell.*" But it sounded fake, and maybe even she thought so. She slumped in her chair like a marionette whose strings had been cut, and shook her head helplessly. I was starting to feel bizarrely guilty. I had come here for a confrontation, to somehow clear the air, not to make anyone else miserable, even someone who seemed to hate me.

"Yes, he did it," she said, smiling in a twisted way, as if the memory were somehow ironic. "He's done other things over the years. To me and to Casey. Though he stopped when Casey got big enough to fight back." She lowered her voice conspiratorially even though we were alone, "Lord forgive me, but at first I thought my husband killed Casey because he announced he wanted to be a teacher, for the love of God, and wanted to educate people, not kill them." She shook her head in disbelief. "Like there's anything better than serving your country?"

"But why is your husband doing this to us *now*?"

"Don't you understand? The anniversary of Casey's death was a few weeks ago," she brought out sadly. Then she flared up: "I didn't think Casey was miserable enough to kill himself, but what did I know? When the autopsy report said it was suicide for sure, that's when I understood."

I was dumbfounded by the ease with which she told a stranger she had suspected her husband of murdering their son.

"So he's abused you and Casey?"

"Yes, and that's why Casey changed his name to mine when he turned eighteen."

"Have you ever reported the abuse?"

She sneered. "To the police? Sonny boy, he *is* the police. He's invulnerable, he's a detective in the Michiganapolis police. Detective Quinn." She explained what she seemed sure I was going to ask: "When we separated, I changed back to my maiden name and when Casey turned eighteen, he took my name, too, because he hated his father. He was right to. My husband is a real snake. That's what you get when you mix Irish blarney and Italian charm."

"What do you mean?" I asked, still not entirely able to absorb what she was revealing to me: we were being stalked and harassed by a *cop*, the very person who was supposed to keep people safe. But then what did that cliché mean anymore, now that I'd experienced police brutality firsthand, and Vanessa Liberati had taken us behind the scenes of what some of the local police were really like.

"What do I mean? His mother's Italian, that's why his first name is Dante." She sneered. "I wanted security, he seemed so solid. I married a man with a first name like that, I ended up in hell right from the get-go. What a crummy joke." She glanced off as if seeing the young woman she'd been before her life had changed for the worse. "It's not just what he did to *us*. He beat up people he arrested, he lied on police reports, stole evidence, and he'd brag about it to me."

But how had she stayed silent so long?

As if she'd read my mind, she said, "Nobody would believe me. He'd tell them I'm a drunk, and that's true. I drink too much. That was the only way I could live with him. Besides, you don't report people like Dante to anyone no matter what they do, you don't tell your friends about him, you don't even tell your minister. My husband, he's—" She seemed to struggle with a description. "He's a *devil*."

If Detective Dante Quinn really was behind everything that had been happening to us, then she wasn't exaggerating. And that's when I remembered Vanessa Liberati asking who was in charge on the night of the raid, and some cop telling her, "Detective Quinn."

I could still barely absorb the revelation and clung to what we'd been talking about, asking her, "But don't people go to prison for spousal abuse?"

She nodded. "They can. Sometimes. And they get released. You don't stay in forever. And *he* would get revenge."

"Then how were you able to manage a separation?"

"That was Dante's idea, for whatever reason. Maybe it was Casey getting big and muscular, able to stand up for himself and for me, that made Dante want to get rid of the both of us. I don't really know and I didn't ask. But I know nobody leaves him, nobody crosses him. He's the one in charge, always. He'll never let me go, never give me a divorce."

"So you're in limbo," I said.

"But at least he's stopped beating on me. Now he has you and your . . . your partner to punish." She shrugged and drank some more tea as if she'd merely made a remark about the weather.

"Why are you telling me all this?"

"Why?" She sneered. "I hate all of you at the college, but I hate him more."

I wondered that she had the university's radio station on at all, given how she felt, unless it was just mindless background noise to her.

"You're telling me there's nothing I can do."

"Oh, you can fix things easy enough," she said calmly after a moment. "You can sell your house and move to another country, because

I guarantee it, if you stay in the U.S. Dante will eventually hurt you real bad, maybe even kill you. He's *that* crazy. And he'll get away with it."

While I tried to assimilate the threat, and wondered if she could possibly be inventing all of what she'd been telling me, or even some of it, she shook her head a bit as if answering to some inner voice. With a show of vestigial hospitality, she asked "Would you like some of these sugar cookies? I baked them myself."

"I have to go."

She nodded, and rose unsteadily to her feet.

"I am truly sorry about your son."

She waved it away. "Too little, too late." By the door was a small console table with a wedding photo. It was clearly her and Quinn. She saw me study it, and said, "He won't let me put it away. He wants me to remember who's the boss every time I come home, and every time I leave."

I took in Quinn, my nemesis. He was much taller than she was, an imposing, square-jawed type with a thick neck, dimpled chin, and dead eyes. Even on his wedding day, he wasn't smiling.

20

In my car, I texted Vanessa that I'd found out it was Detective Quinn behind the last week of horror, and then I drove straight to campus to tell Stefan the astonishing story Quinn's estranged wife had revealed to me.

But could I believe Pat Silver? Hadn't Stefan told me Casey said both his parents were harsh?

Upstairs, when I exited the elevator on the third floor, I could see Stefan standing in the doorway of Celine's office, off to the left across that small sea of low-walled cubicle partitions. There were only a few bent heads among the warren of desks, and once again, it struck me as a remarkable and bizarre reversal in my departmental fortunes that I wasn't among them. But I knew from Shakespeare that Fortune's Wheel could turn sharply, and hadn't it done just that only days ago?

Estella was dressed in clinging pink and black Lycra today like an aerobics instructor. She smiled absently as I passed, though whether at me or her smart phone where she was texting, I couldn't say. Stefan waved, and as I skirted the cubicles and got closer, I could see he was talking to Celine who stood just inside the doorway of her office. I greeted them both. She was wearing a lime green cottony outfit almost like loose pajamas. She looked cool, but she said with an unusual hint of shyness, "A nephew of mine is in the Iowa writing program and a really big fan of memoirs, so he wanted me to get him a signed copy of Stefan's book."

Stefan grinned as he always did (and probably always would) at any mention of his only best-selling book. He pulled a copy out of his black leather Ferragamo messenger bag. This was also the only book of his with an author photo plastered across the back cover, a sign of how well the publisher had thought the book would do.

"Are you sure I can't pay you for it?" Celine asked him.

He nodded.

"Listen," I said, voice low, since the echo on this newly redesigned floor was unpredictable, "you are not going to believe what I just found out." I ushered them both into Celine's office, and shut the heavy oak door behind me. It closed with a thud.

Celine sat down behind her desk, Stefan on the deep, cushioned windowsill, setting his bag on the floor at his feet.

I paced back and forth as I recounted everything Quinn's wife had told me: their contempt for all of us at SUM, his abuse, her suspecting him of killing Casey, her conviction that he was our tormentor. Stefan was still, back straight, brawny arms folded, but his eyes got wider and wider. When I was done, Celine nodded almost as if she had suspected this revelation.

"Nothing the po-po does surprises me," she said. I knew that was African American slang for the police, like "5-o." "I can't begin to count how many times my eldest son has gotten stopped around here because his Daddy splurged and gave him an Audi A3 for his eighteenth birthday."

"Driving While Black," Stefan muttered.

Celine nodded. "And you two, no matter what somebody thinks you did or didn't do, you're gay and that puts you way down the totem pole no matter what happens. You can't tell me that isn't part of all this shit that's been going down. It's not just that you're professors."

I'd never heard Celine use even mild profanity before, or slang. I was about to ask her more about her son when I noticed Stefan had turned and was staring out the window.

"There are people running down there," he said, frowning. "Something must be happening. A car accident?"

We hadn't heard any crash, so I doubted that.

Celine and I moved to the window, and I realized that the people were running *out of* Parker Hall and scattering in all directions. But there hadn't been any fire alarm, so what was going on? Some of them had stopped across the street and were on their smart phones, making calls and gesticulating wildly with their free hands. Others were pointing, taking pictures with their phones. But pictures of what?

That's when we heard muffled shouting from somewhere in the building and another sound I couldn't identify. We all stood there, frozen, holding our breath, as if somehow being utterly still could magically protect us. Then I heard that weird clanging echo of the stairs, and from the office below us, there was a terrifically loud, bizarre grinding and shaking that rattled the framed Hitchcock posters on Celine's walls.

"The copy room is right below us," Celine said. "I think someone's trying to move one of the copy machines." Celine's forehead creased in puzzlement.

Stefan and I asked "Why?" at the same time.

"To blockade the door."

"From what?" Stefan asked.

That's when we heard what I was sure was a gun shot, and a scream. Both of them traveled up through the floor the way dark spirits swoop into and out of people in horror films. I felt just as shaken and hollowed out. I waited for something to fill the emptiness: memories, visions, anything.

"It's Quinn," Stefan said dully. "It's got to be Quinn. He probably followed you to his wife's house, or maybe she even told him you were there after you left. How do you know she's not as crazy as he is?"

"This is not possible," I said. "This is not happening."

Celine was on her cell. As she dialed 911, she said, "I don't think we can get out of here. We're too high up to jump and we could get caught on the stairs or in the elevator."

I listened to her efficiently and calmly report who and where we were, what we had heard and what we thought was going on. After she finished, she told me and Stefan, "They're getting other calls about a gunman and that at least one person's been shot. Campus is being evacuated. They told us to hide and protect ourselves as best we can if we can't escape."

I felt as if I had silently shrunk into myself, and all I could picture was the first of the Twin Towers imploding and collapsing, sending up a mountain of dust and ash. We were going to die as surely as everyone who couldn't get out of those buildings had died. Quinn would find us and he was going to kill us. It was over.

I could suddenly hear my breathing: short and fast. My chest felt tight and there was a strange tension at the back of my throat as if I were about to start choking. Despite what Celine had said, I wanted to try jumping from one of the windows, but then I pictured myself breaking one or both legs and lying there unable to move, helpless, an easier target than I was already.

Celine grabbed my arm and shook me hard. "Nick! Stay focused." I looked at her as if I were at the bottom of a pool and she was dragging me to the surface. Then I saw that Stefan's lips were moving and I could just make out that he was praying the "Hail Mary." And that's when it hit me: Maybe I was going to die, but I wouldn't die alone. We were together. And perhaps that could save us somehow, but my thinking had slowed down as if I were drugged.

I nodded at Celine anyway, to show that I wasn't giving up.

She stalked through the connecting doorway into my office, closed and locked my outer door to the rest of the department, then passed back through the connecting doorway to rejoin me and Stefan, closing that door behind her.

"Your office is closest to the elevator," she said. "And if he breaks in that way, he'll probably come through *there*." She pointed at the door between our offices. She whirled around and started scrabbling in her desk. "Damn. I never lock that door, I don't know where the key is." Then she smacked her forehead, reached into her skirt pocket and pulled out her keychain, found the large brass key, locked the connecting door and sighed as deeply as if she'd just finished a marathon.

She locked her other door, then glanced around the room, clearly trying to figure out what we could move in front of the connecting door to slow Quinn down or even stop him. But he'd find us eventually.

"Help me with that book case!" she said to us, pointing at the four-foot-tall metal book case behind her desk. Stefan and I got on one side and slid it across in front of the door between our offices. Some of the binders and books toppled out of it onto the floor, lying splayed open like corpses in a morgue. Stefan grabbed her desk chair and stacked it on top of the bookcase, then added the only other chair in the room and a small three-legged table that had stood under the window and held a philodendron. It wasn't much, but the door was also one of the old, heavy, recycled doors from before the building renovation and maybe would gain us some time till the police came.

The Michiganapolis police. They'd ruined my life, ruined Stefan's life just a week ago, and now we were waiting for them to save us. It was terrifying. One of their own had started this whole nightmare and was in the building determined to kill us and who knew how many other people. It had to be Quinn, who else would be going berserk like this?

All three of us were staring at Celine's office door out to the department now, and then we circled the room for anything big enough to make a barricade for this one, too. We tried moving the file cabinet standing to its left, but it was too heavy to slide and if we just tipped it over on its side, it wouldn't do much to keep anyone out. Her old oak desk didn't budge. Even if we'd pulled out the desk drawers I didn't think we could maneuver the desk onto one end and ram it against the door.

Celine shook her head. "Okay, stay away from the door, anyway. The bullets penetrate much easier than through a wall, even these old walls."

"How do you know that?" I asked, making sure I did what she said.

"They train us for emergencies like this. We just have to hold out somehow till the cops get here. But we need weapons. If he gets in, we have to try to disarm or disable him."

Her assurance calmed me down, but I cursed myself for not having moved faster after that terrible first night to apply for a gun license and buy a gun. If only I had a gun, any kind of gun, we'd truly be able to defend ourselves.

Celine surveyed the office again, and yanked the fire extinguisher from its wall mount behind her desk. It wasn't much, but it was something. I lifted the *Psycho* poster from its spot near the door, turned it glass side out and figured that if she and I and Stefan hit Quinn at the same time, maybe we'd have a chance. It was heavier than I'd expected, and could possibly do enough damage to buy us the time we needed.

But just as I was wondering what Stefan could use to try to disarm Quinn, I saw him bending over his messenger bag, and then he pulled out a handgun. I thought I recognized it from one of the brochures I had been reading: it looked like a Walther PPK .380, but different from the ones I'd seen in catalogues, and it had what I guessed was a custom wrap-around grip of some fancy wood. I watched Stefan check to see that it was unloaded, grab ammo from a small cardboard box, take out the magazine, carefully but quickly load it and slide it in, then click off the safety as smoothly as if he'd handled it many times. He was ready.

I no longer recognized this man, and I didn't know what to say. Celine was silent, too. Time seemed to stop. No, that wasn't it. *We* had stopped. We stood at the dead center of a ravenous storm whirling around us.

He met my eyes, unabashed. "Those times this past week I haven't been around? Father Ryan took me out to a friend's farm to try out a bunch of different handguns. He knew how scared I was. This was the one that I got off the best shots with." Stefan was holding the PPK safely, pointing it down to the floor, but the image of him with any kind of gun was surreal. "Nick," he said, "I'm not going to die without fighting back." And before I could say anything, he added, "No, I don't have a license to carry it. I don't have any kind of license and I don't give a fuck."

I didn't either. "But why didn't you want me to have a gun?"

He shrugged. "You're too combustible."

I would have laughed if we weren't in so much danger. It didn't matter that he had berated me when we had talked about gun permits after Vanessa Liberati had urged us to protect ourselves. I was grateful that at least one of us had a real weapon, and adjectives from the Walther website I had once taken a look at drifted through my mind as if I were hallucinating: "classic," "timeless," "elegant." They seemed obscenely frivolous now that we were about to face a maniac, words that were better suited to a fashion show. The PPK was small as semiautomatics went (six inches long, about four inches high), and I'd read somewhere that it was worthless for self-defense. I hoped to God that wasn't true.

I nodded at Stefan, still speechless, but I think we had lived together long enough for him to know that I was commending him.

Stefan nodded back, grimly, then waved me and Celine with our makeshift weapons to the right side of the massive door. To the left was the gray metal file cabinet like millions of others across the country, one that we had tried to move but couldn't, not that it would have made much difference since it was much narrower than the door. Stefan crouched down next to it. If the door gave way, it might block Quinn's view—for a moment.

"How many rounds?" I asked Stefan, unable for some reason to recall the PPK's capacity.

"Seven."

Seven chances. But not with a better gun like a Glock or Sig Sauer. . . .

"Can he get through the door?" Celine wondered. And then she answered her own question in a murmur: "All he has to do is shoot out the lock."

We weren't hiding inside a bank vault. As heavy and thick as it was, the door was just an office door.

It was very cool in Celine's office but my forehead and neck were sweaty and the room seemed filled with whatever floral perfume Celine was wearing.

I heard the distinctive ding of the elevator and then someone bellowed "Where are those faggots?"

It was followed by a scream, the *boom* of a gunshot, then a shout of "Get back here you bitch!" and a second shot. The echoes in that high-ceilinged space were tremendous and the blasts were as loud as anything I'd ever heard in a movie—and far more terrifying. I closed my eyes and almost dropped the framed poster whose sides I was gripping, but Celine hissed at me, "Get ready!"

On the far side of the door, I heard Stefan breathing even harder than I was. And then the far-off ululating sirens of police cars came blasting up around us with the force of a gale, and I was sure I could hear the distinctive rumble of a fire truck. Was I imagining it, or had all those vehicle engines made the building shake a little?

Maybe we'd survive. Maybe they'd storm the building before he could get to us.

Stefan moved quickly to the window, wisely keeping his gun out of sight. "There are five cop cars down there and they're already setting up barricades to keep people back. The crowd's enormous. Some of the cops are crouching down behind the cars."

It had sounded like more than five cars to me, and must have been, because from what seemed like the other side of the building, a distorted voice crackled over a megaphone: "Drop your weapon and come out with your hands up before anyone else gets hurt."

They didn't know exactly where he was, I thought.

Stefan stepped back to his spot by the filing cabinet. Celine murmured to me, "Get ready, I think they're going into hostage mode. It's on us now."

"Does he *have* hostages?"

She shrugged and turned her head back toward the door. We heard more screams out there, partitions crashing, chairs falling over. I was briefly glad that the main directory with all our names and office numbers we had before the renovations hadn't been replaced, but that wouldn't buy us much time. There were only six offices with name-plates on this floor, and I knew he had found us when Stefan's door crashed open. Posters rattled on the wall between Celine's office and Stefan's, and everything else in the office we'd locked ourselves into shuddered.

Celine flinched and Stefan ducked down as if he were actually in his office just a few feet away.

Cursing and smashing followed on the other side of the wall. Quinn was probably enraged that the office was empty. There was another crash and I saw a laptop hurtle past our window and down to shatter below. Police outside fired up at the building. We all dropped to the floor and I almost rolled onto the framed poster as we heard shots burying themselves in the soft sandstone walls before someone shouted from outside "Cease fire! Cease fire, you morons!"

Quinn didn't fire back and we could hear his heavy tread heading toward us, to where we were waiting for the final confrontation. It had to be final. Either *he* died, or *we* did.

I felt very stiff, as if I'd been locked inside a cold storage unit. I stood up, grabbing the poster, and planted myself firmly right next to Celine who held the fire extinguisher like an axe. She suddenly changed her position, lowering it to her chest. She pulled out the pin that locked the operating handled, telling me, "I'll spray him in the face and try to blind him. Then *you* hit him with Hitchcock."

I peered out from behind the poster and saw that Stefan had just resumed his crouching position, the gun firmly in both hands, his knees slightly bent, his arms extended.

The door thumped as if a furious beast had rammed into it. The pounding came again. And again.

"*He's kicking the door in,*" I whispered, unable to imagine the kind of fury that would make someone do that.

The door shuddered again and again. Then the brass door plate and knob flew off as the battered door burst open in a shower of wood splinters, smashing against the file cabinet where Stefan was waiting but now invisible to me. I was frozen and expected to die in that very instant.

Breathing loudly through his mouth, a colossus in black stepped into the room, filling my vision. The man's sharp profile told me it was definitely Quinn. He was easily six feet two and well over two hundred pounds of muscle and rage armored in black boots, pants, t-shirt, wool hat. He held a big black gun that looked like a Glock 20. How many rounds did he have left?

Quinn was standing only a few feet from us, but before Celine or I could make any kind of move to try to stop him, we heard a gunshot from off beyond the door. Quinn grunted and stumbled forward one step. As if part of me were an architect studying blueprints, I realized that Stefan must have shot Quinn in the back and the bullet had probably hit one of his ribs, driving him forward from the waist and knocking him off balance. But why wasn't he wearing a protective vest?

Before Quinn could straighten up and turn, Stefan stepped forward and shot him in the back of the head. The black-clad figure toppled to the floor, knees first. Then his head crashed down and hit the uncarpeted tile flooring with a grotesque cracking sound that made me gag.

The Glock had slipped from Quinn's hands as he fell, sliding across the floor and under Celine's desk. I waited for it to go off like a bomb, even though I knew it wouldn't. My face and hands were wet with sweat or tears, my ears filled with the roar of my own pulse—or was it the two rounds Stefan had fired?

The framed poster started to slide from my hands and I grabbed it tightly before the glass could shatter, leaned it carefully against the wall behind me, wiping my hands on my jeans, afraid now to look at our persecutor, even though he had to be dead. In my mind, the door seemed to be crashing open over and over.

Another shot followed, making me jump.

I looked up to see Stefan standing close to the prone body, his face cold and implacable. Holding the Walther in both hands, he fired into Quinn's back four more times, emptying his gun. Quinn hadn't shown any signs of life after his head smashed onto the floor, but I didn't think of telling Stefan to stop. I was too stunned to say anything, and each spent cartridge flipping out of his gun and clattering on the floor was like the lash of a whip.

Quinn's body seemed to jerk a bit with the impact of each shot—unless I was imagining it, wishing for it—and I felt a sour taste in my mouth. Blood had seeped onto the floor from Quinn's nose or mouth. I wasn't sure which.

My ears were ringing, and the very faint haze left by Stefan's gun irritated my eyes.

I had never before seen anyone killed right in front of me, and Quinn's lifeless body looked as massive as the toppled statue of a dictator. The room stank, filled with the acrid tang of gunpowder and what I realized was the metallic reek of my sweat-soaked clothes. I felt trapped inside a new nightmare.

"Sweet Jesus," Celine murmured.

I heard moaning outside of the office, out amid the cubicles, but I couldn't move to help anyone at the moment. The supine corpse loomed in front of me like a cliff wall, enormous, forbidding. I didn't see how I could ever get around it.

Stefan's lips were moving, but this time he wasn't praying. Voice breaking, he said, "Father Ryan— He told me—"

"Told you what?" I asked.

As if speaking from a distance, Stefan murmured, "'Don't hesitate. Keep shooting.'"

Celine shook herself, set aside the fire extinguisher, headed around Quinn's corpse to the window, yanked it up and yelled to the cops below, "He's dead."

Celine turned to Stefan, who was trembling now, eyes shut. She walked over, touched his shoulder with one hand and his arm with the other, and said quietly, as if comforting an anxious child in a thunderstorm, "You can put the gun down now, honey."

Epilogue

The toll at Parker Hall was five dead, one wounded. Quinn had killed two history professors on the first floor near the entrance, one of whom had tried to tackle him after the other was shot. On the floor below ours, he'd shot a graduate student before he could successfully barricade himself in the copy room. On our floor, he had killed poor, texting Estella and shot Juno Dromgoole in the shoulder as she was trying to hide amid the cubicles. That's who had been moaning. The other few faculty who had been in the cubicles escaped being shot, but one suffered a stroke during the ordeal and was unlikely to recover.

The fifth fatality was Quinn himself.

When the police raided Quinn's apartment in downtown Michiganapolis, they found a scene right out of a stalker movie: a room where an entire wall was papered with articles and photographs of Stefan and me, both together and individually. There was also a crazy diary in which he'd made all kinds of elaborate plans to destroy us, including the call that set the SWAT team on us. There wasn't any hint, though, of why he hadn't worn a police vest on his killing spree, and whether or not he expected to be arrested or killed. A police investigation was launched, but I had no hopes it would be definitive or even a hundred percent truthful.

Had his wife called Quinn after I left her house to have him follow me? Or was he keeping tabs on her? Or simply following me again? We'd never know. All I cared about was that we were free. The persecution was over.

Despite killing a cop, Stefan became a national hero overnight because the headlines dubbed Quinn a "psycho." A bill to commend Stefan for defending himself was introduced in the state legislature, but quickly quashed by the governor, who obviously thought any more attention to the story would hurt tourism in our state.

Stefan wisely refused to do any media interviews, which may have been one reason why the district attorney did not charge him with anything, not even carrying a concealed weapon. That particular part of the story was successfully kept quiet. I'm sure the university's lawyers and PR people worked overtime on suppressing whatever they could, and no reporters bothered to investigate whether Stefan's gun was his or if he had a license to carry. And outside of the police, nobody but me, Celine, Stefan, and Father Ryan knew the provenance of the gun that he'd used to kill Quinn.

The Walther PPK was off the books, had never been registered. It was a war souvenir that Father Ryan's grandfather had brought back from Germany in 1945, and was actually worth several thousand dollars because it was in excellent condition. I don't know if the converted-to-Catholicism son of Holocaust survivors defending himself with what might have been a Nazi's gun he obtained from a priest is ironic, or just bizarre. I guess it doesn't matter.

Everyone wanted the story to disappear. But if there *had* been a trial, most likely for second-degree murder because Stefan had killed a cop, he would have had an unlikely assortment of defenders aside from Vanessa Liberati: everyone from the NRA to the ACLU, since both organizations were among the many that issued public statements praising his heroism. The ACLU used his story to call for more gun control, and the NRA used it to call for arming all university professors. Stefan could have been the darling of Fox News *and* MSNBC.

A trial would have brought protest marches and demonstrations and Facebook pages dedicated to his acquittal, and t-shirts and bumper stickers and endless tweeting. That kind of publicity would have made Michiganapolis and the university look terrible. And possibly hurt St. Jude Church and Father Ryan as well.

The publicity storm based on what *was* known led to Stefan's memoir hitting the best-seller lists all over again.

Right after the SWAT raid, Father Ryan had suggested we take a cruise or trip to get away from the scene and clear our minds, and that was even better advice now. It was the height of summer, but we decided to escape to Europe anyway despite the hordes of other tourists we'd likely encounter. Marco stayed with Binnie down the street for a month while we made our leisurely way from Venice to Nice to Bruges, soaking up sun, wine, and culture. Stefan relished the churches, I favored the museums; we both adored the food, and Stefan with his good ear for languages picked up an amazing amount of both Italian and Flemish, which startled the natives who couldn't believe he was from the U.S.

Traveling Americans sometimes recognized Stefan from covers of *Time* and *Newsweek*, but if anyone did try to get him talking about the "Michigan Massacre," we walked away. Near the end of our vacation, dining on Belgian beef stew, we discussed writing books about what had happened. He's still thinking about his.

Mine, of course, is done.

If you enjoyed this book, please review it online. Even a short review makes a difference and would be appreciated. Word-of-mouth is crucial in publishing.

You can read what Lev has to say about writing and publishing at his blog "Writing Across Genres" (http://www.levraphael.com/blog/).

Feel free to drop by and chat. You can also follow Lev on Twitter (https://twitter.com/LevRaphael) or Facebook (https://www.facebook.com/levraphael).

To send him an email, go to his website (http://www.levraphael.com).

Author's Note

Mary Chantier, Owen Deatrick, and Mike Peplowski were invaluable in my research for this book, answering many legal, forensic, and weapons-related questions for me. I'm deeply grateful for their time and expertise.

Also by Lev Raphael

Fiction

Dancing on Tisha B'Av
Winter Eyes
The German Money
Secret Anniversaries of the Heart
Rosedale in Love
Pride and Prejudice: The Jewess and the Gentile
The Vampyre of Gotham

Mysteries

Let's Get Criminal
The Edith Wharton Murders
The Death of a Constant Lover
Little Miss Evil
Burning Down the House
Tropic of Murder
Hot Rocks

Nonfiction

Edith Wharton's Prisoners of Shame
Journeys & Arrivals
Writing a Jewish Life
My Germany
Book Lust!
Writer's Block Is Bunk

Coauthored

Dynamics of Power
Coming Out of Shame
Stick Up for Yourself!
Stick Up for Yourself! Teacher's Guide

31901067062374